WILD HEART

BY

TISH HAND

ISBN: 1-4033-3887-6 (e-book)
ISBN: 1-4033-3888-4 (Paperback)
ISBN: 1-4033-3889-2 (Dustjacket)

Library of Congress Control Number: 2002092359

This book is printed on acid free paper.

Printed in the United States of America
Bloomington, IN

1stBooks - rev. 09/16/02

CHAPTER ONE

"Amy, regardless of your motives, it's still meddling. I'm not ready for Tom, Dick, and Harry, let alone some new, handsome lawyer named Greg Seever. You go out with him. My plans are laid, and I'm not going to change them at this late date."

"Oh, Deedee, can't you see you're just running away from your problems. You need your friends more than ever right now. And you have no business traipsing off to some godforsaken hole on the side of a mountain. You haven't ever so much as taken a hike. It's suicidal. Is that what you're intending?"

"Absolutely not." Deedee felt sorry for the poor woman whose voice raised in desperation for Deedee. Why did it matter so much? Why had Amy been so solicitous of Deedee since her husband's death? It didn't make sense. They just had never been that tight. In the tradition of close Arizona neighborhoods, Amy was an acquaintance, but little more. Why had she become so adamant to mold Deedee's life? "You're the one killing me…with kindness," she clarified. "There's only one cure for this wound, and that's my work."

"But you said you haven't been able to write. What makes you think Colorado will change that?"

"Because, Amy, I can't do my work while weeding through the garden of love my well-meaning friends are planting to mire my feet. I can't think. I can't concentrate. My God, I can't even dream."

Deedee offered Amy a frustrated glare along with the tall glass of lemonade she carefully placed on the crystal and silver coaster. Drawing in a deep sigh, she released her body to the blood red, leather couch. So, she had shocked her friend into silence; the peace was bliss, though short-lived.

Deedee had drunk half of her glass of cool refreshment before she set it aside. The hot Arizona day had sapped her of her fluids and her spirits during the short talk that resurrected the haunting memories of the past. She had seen Amy follow Daniel into the kitchen when he went for beer. It had been far too long before they returned flush and giggling like children. Daniel had accidently bumped against her when he bent to open the cooler. That very day, four months ago, Deedee's whole world had shattered with the unexpected death of her husband.

With no warning, no long illness, no doctors, no hospitals, Daniel lost his life. He had been handsome, athletic, and loving, besides patient with the understanding he had shown when Deedee was so drawn in by her writing she failed to cook his meals or even go to his bed.

Was Amy really killing Deedee with kindness because of her own deeply-seated guilt? Yes, that must be the answer. What would have happened had not Daniel died at his fortieth birthday party? Deedee didn't believe Daniel had cheated on her, but he had been very restless about passing such a landmark in his life. Her only clues were his constant questions about his physique and his performance in bed. Regardless of her assurances, too many hours were spent in front of the mirror instead of in the bed. Hoping a party would help, Deedee had invited everyone they knew, including his business associates and friends on the block.

Amy's whining voice broke her reverie, so different from the coquettish, low drone she used when men were near. "Who will take care of you, Deedee? Who will be there to make sure you eat? There isn't even a telephone where you're going. How can you do this?! It's insane!"

"I'll have Cisco and Poncho with me. Right now, they're all the company I can handle."

"Do you expect that Poodle and ferret to protect you in the wild? You need a Great Dane!"

"Oh, for Pete's sake. Amy, listen, I hate to be rude, but I have an awful lot to do before I leave. I'll run to get the bonsai you promised to babysit."

Deedee carried the little tree she had planted to honor the sale of her first book fifteen years earlier from the place of honor it held on her spacious back porch. It signified her whole career; each ring of new wood marking one more year she remained independent in her life and earnings. Superstition dictated that she would lose these precarious things if this little tree were to die; practicality dictated the ridiculousness of superstition. Still, she felt a sense of loss when she handed it lovingly to Amy.

"Remember, morning sun only and water it when the moss starts to dry. This is precious to me, Amy. Please don't let it die."

"You've had quite enough death. I wouldn't dream of it." Slapping her hand to her mouth, she apologized. "Leave it to me to say the wrong thing. Sorry. That's all you need— someone to keep reminding you."

"Don't be silly. There isn't a moment, day or night, when I forget it. I only hope I'm so lucky when it's my time to go. Daniel didn't even make a sound. He couldn't have felt much pain. Sometimes I feel that I've suffered his death more than he did, and it shows me my selfishness. But one minute he was turning the hamburgers and the next he was gone."

"I know, Deedee. I was there. No one would have believed it otherwise." Her nosy neighbor mind ticking like a cuckoo clock, Amy needled for more info. "If it doesn't bother you to talk about it, what did the doctor say was the cause of death?"

No doubt, the question came out of guilt that, possibly, her own lurid activities had caused his demise. Amy probably thought Deedee poisoned him for being unfaithful. Well, let her think what she would. It had provided an edge of intrigue to their visits. Deedee was certain an affair had never happened, but she was just as certain that it soon would have. Not because they were having marital problems but because he needed affirmation of his sexual prowess with women when he "WENT OVER THE HILL". For some reason, wives don't qualify in that endeavor. Deedee didn't blame Amy. If it hadn't been her, it would have been another neighbor or a secretary—female flesh to make his forty-year-old body feel twenty again.

"It was simply heart failure. He had a heart murmur as a child, and he worked at a high-stress job. Corporate law was worse than being a doctor. He was always on call."

Sighing, Deedee turned to stare out the window at the harsh sun. She heard Amy clear her throat, suggestively, at her long silence.

"Poor Deedee," Amy said. "We could have had great fun together this summer. Look how much we have in common: both of us are now single and attractive, and neither of us has children. With no children and no husbands, we would be footloose and fancy-free. Boy, the men we could meet."

With no response forthcoming from the moody Deedee, Amy continued her ranting lecture. "Where are your priorities? Don't they even include men? I find that odd because your novels exude lust and promiscuity. Where do the words come from? Do you want to live your life inside the pages of a book? I've tried everything to get you out of the house. You refuse every invitation to every party, say no to every date I try to arrange. You remain a zombie in this coffin of a house. Now you want to lose herself in the woods on the pretext of work. Maybe you need more time, Deedee, but I doubt it. You've always been a homebody who seems perfectly content whacking away at a typewriter, or grooming your poodle, or digging dirt in your garden. I can't bear to sit at home. I much prefer parties, or shopping, or dancing, or…anything that will get me out of the house. My house is strictly utilitarian—a place to sleep and change my clothes."

"You're being rude. Let alone loquacious."

"'Loquacious?' God, that's just what I mean. That's a word for a book, not for real life. Why won't you listen to reason? Do you want to become a total hermit locked inside your computer screen? Do you want to dig a hole and pull the ground in over you? When you come back with a total mental breakdown, maybe you'll be more apt to heed my advice and I will gladly say, I told you so."

"Enough. Enough, Amy. Shoo. I have to pack and close up. I'll stop by for coffee on my way out in the morning."

Deedee manhandled her toward the door while reassuring Amy's firm grip on the little tree. "Oh, I nearly forgot." Digging through the tiny drawer in the foyer, she came up with her find. "Here's the key in case of an emergency. Ms Bradley will collect the mail and water the garden."

Deedee cringed when Amy tripped on the step.

* * * * * * *

Cisco stuck his nose into the tiny crack of the car window and danced on Deedee's lap for solid purchase. He tried to inhale the whole desert sky. Poncho bumped the seat beneath her, exploring the deeper recesses of this new, delightful, hiding place. The parched July ground whizzed by while mirage pools evaporated in rays of heat waves on the white, white highway.

Amy had continued to plead her case while Cisco had yapped, to hurry, from the car. There had been no time for coffee. The thermometer had read ninety-five and rising by the time Deedee had fastened down the door on the little trailer. She had persuaded Amy to stand behind the trailer to check the lights and signals, and then Deedee had waved good-by to the startled woman.

Feeling a little remorse for leaving so abruptly, Deedee was, nonetheless, anxious to distance herself from Amy. Amy did mean well, but they were nothing alike. Amy was a femme fatale. All of the men drooled at her short dresses and bikinis. She sucked up the attention like a floundering fish gasps for air and with the same pucker. Deedee dressed for comfort. She had the body: never stretched by childbirth, never inflated by leisure. Whether mentally or physically, Deedee was always motivated. When her body rested, her mind worked. When her mind rested, her body worked. She had just never felt the need to flaunt her figure before men.

There was no doubt that her long marriage had made her feel secure in her appeal to the opposite sex. When her words aroused her from the pages of the love stories she wrote, Daniel had always been there to fill her needs. (When he had been home.) Their work hours hadn't always meshed and rare was the night they retired together, but their catch-up time had been well spent.

Yes, she missed him terribly. Married after her high school graduation, Deedee had spent her entire life with the man. If she hadn't become so independent in her interests, she wouldn't have been able to go on after his death.

Everything she enjoyed was contained in her home and yard. She made required trips to her publisher and an occasional book signing, only to return to the things she loved. The grocery store, or bakery, or drugstore were unwanted, but necessary, distractions. She forced herself to the kitchen when her stomach protested in loud roars of her neglect.

Amy had made one comment that plagued Deedee. Though she tried to dismiss it with the same flippancy with which she dismissed most of Amy's thoughts, this one persisted in tormenting her. "Deedee," Amy had said, "why don't you DO instead of WRITE?"

Hurt and confused, the more Deedee thought about it, the more hurt and confused she became. The ridiculous statement was whittling away at her very existence and self-esteem. Amy acted as if Deedee had no life at all—as if her novels replaced real life. Was it the truth of the statement that kept it ever present in Deedee's mind?

Dancing from one cracked window to the other and threatening high-speed death, Cisco demanded attention to his need for a short walk. This, at least, was real life. Deedee pulled over to the berm and fished for the leash, while checking Poncho's whereabouts. The back seat litter box would alleviate one of her worries.

Cars screamed by as she forged through the one hundred and five degree heat to find a sticker/cactus free spot to put Cisco down in. He squirmed in readiness. After he finished, Deedee was still faced with pulling several burrs from his soft, black fuzz before he could get into the car.

She wolfed down a sandwich from a paper bag and shared five cookies with her critters. Having poured the icy water from a thermos into the dog dish on the floorboard, Deedee drank from the wide lid while Cisco and Poncho greedily lapped their fill. Thus refreshed, in a matter of minutes, she eased her little car back into traffic. Unable to leave her animals to suffer in the heat, Deedee had given up the idea of cafe cuisine.

They were doing pretty well for their first road trip. She had always boarded them in the past but couldn't bear to leave them behind now. The love they gave her, in profusion, had helped her through many lonely hours.

Should she sell the big, empty house? It seemed so ostentatious to her without Daniel's presence. It had had to be so to impress his elite clients and to entertain his employers. It had well suited Daniel, but, without him, it was excess baggage. Everything she cared about would fit in two small rooms. No, everything she cared about had fit into the four-by-four foot trailer behind her car.

She had only seen a fuzzy newspaper picture of the one room log cabin she was moving into, for God knows how long. It was clouded by pine trees and shade, but the big patio, hanging out over infinity, had sold her. The sliding glass door looked like an anomaly in the rustic setting, but it gave her comfort. It would remind her of the era so she wouldn't lose her path back to reality.

Luck had been with her when she called the realtor to obtain the property. It had long been deserted by the aged couple who had enjoyed it in their youth. The realtor had made arrangements for repairs, and even after the electrical and water hookups, the price had been reasonable. Her only inconvenience would be the wood burning stove and the lack of a telephone. A hot plate would solve the former, and it couldn't be that far into Green Mountain Falls?

Cisco, reaching the end of his endurance, stretched across her lap and closed his dark eyes. Poncho continued to scratch at some unknown trinket stuck under the rails of the seat, and Deedee determined to discover the plot of her new book. Her publisher was being very patient, under the circumstances, but she longed to lose herself in another fantasy, if she only could. And to hell with Amy.

The miles began to hypnotize her as Poncho settled to sleep. But Cisco pulled her out of her reverie when he awoke violently and lost his cookies.

Deedee had no idea the seven-hour drive to Albuquerque would take her nine hours. At least she had passed the halfway point.

She decided to stop at a drive-in to have a substantial meal while she contemplated whether to go on driving through the night or to stop and search for a motel that would accept pets. As it was, it would be the wee hours of the morning when she arrived at the cabin.

Cisco and Poncho had slowed her progress by poopy stops, and wrestling stops, and carsick stops. She could still smell the sweet, vomit odor rising up to her from her lap. Certainly, she could take the time to don a clean pair of shorts in a filling-station rest room.

Pulling into an ancient relic with rounded pumps, she hoped to get a cheaper price. No such luck. The gasoline prices, as usual, seemed to be conspiratorial.

Cisco bounced in the back window while she dug through a suitcase in the trunk. Always thinking of comfort before beauty, she pulled a baggy pair of shorts from the folded piles.

The teenager, pumping gas, was making goo-goo eyes at her. His eyebrows were contorting like weird, wild, flying wings, and it looked like one side of his face was at war with the other. Deedee snickered under her breath and asked for directions to the ladies' room.

She fetched the paddle board key and entered the polka-dot room. The white enamel was pocked with age, but it seemed clean regardless of the chipped surfaces.

Slipping off her soiled slacks, Deedee looked down. "Oh no," she grumbled. She had forgotten underwear. The ones she wore were stiff with dried vomit. "Oh well" She pulled off the soiled clothing, cleaned herself with wet paper towels, and pulled on the baggy shorts. Unlike Amy's, her shorts were long and modest. No one would suspect the absence of panties.

Returning the key to its rusted nail, she asked the young man for directions to the best drive-in in town while she paid him over the oily counter. He told her and grabbed her hand provocatively when she passed him the cash. Deedee simply smiled and said, "Thanks." She hurried to leave the station, a little flattered that a man? so young could find her attractive.

Cisco attacked her in wet, licking welcome, and Poncho popped out of her makeup case with a tube of lipstick in his teeth. Deedee lunged to retrieve it before it disappeared, forever, in whatever new hidy hole Poncho had found to stash it in. Patting him and rubbing his arching neck, sorry for his loss, she pushed lipstick and wallet in her purse and zipped it shut.

She should have known better than to take the recommendations of a teenager. Driving into the crowded drive-in, Deedee was deafened by blaring, booming stereos—each battling to blow out windows with deep bass beats. She found a stall at the end of the row large enough to accommodate her car and trailer.

After placing her order, Deedee couldn't tell if the voice on the intercom had gotten it right when he repeated it back to her. She couldn't hear a thing. She quickly rolled her window up to block the noisome racket.

Fearing the car would overheat with the air-conditioning running in idle, she had shut down the engine. The cool interior wouldn't last long.

The order came swiftly, surprising her. Deedee gasped and opened the window to the summer heat. Handing the skating carhop the empty thermos, Deedee asked if she would please refill it. The carhop took the proffered thermos, willingly, and zoomed back to the glass building.

Opening a can of prime dog food and placing the contents in the dog dish on the floorboard, Deedee tried to entice her pets to eat before she dug into her foot-long chili dog and fries. Poncho started eating right away, but Cisco sniffed at the dog food and jumped back up beside her with his paw pointing at the paper-wrapped aroma. He cocked his head and stared at the people food in sad appeal.

"No, Cisco! There's your dinner!"

He flinched from her scolding and laid down on the seat but continued to ogle her chili dog the whole time she was eating.

Two bites later the thermos arrived, clinking with ice and water. Deedee tipped the carhop for the extra effort and hurriedly closed the window—too late. She was sweltering. Her shirt was clinging to her back, plastered with sweat. Restarting the car to re-cool the interior, Deedee ate her meal.

When she reached the last two inches of the foot-long, the hot light blinked and then blared at her in bright red glory. Seconds later STOP ENGINE flashed. "Damn!!"

She pulled the hood release and skinnied out through the narrow door opening. Why had she parked so close to the intercom? Cisco was making courageous attempts to reach the last of the hot dog she had shoved up on the dash.

Lifting the hood, she saw smoke and steam billow out in hissing heat. This would cost her at least an hour of travel time while she waited for her engine to cool. Her problems drew the young people like slivers of metal to a magnet. They all wanted to help. Radios were turned off or down. A hose mysteriously appeared, gushing water.

Cisco barked belligerently at the strangers surrounding his master, forgetting the remnants of her food.

They gave the engine a good hosing down until the cap could be removed, then gave the car a thirst-quenching drink or water. After thanking the helpful teens, Deedee got back into her car. She broke up the last of her hot dog and fries for Cisco, putting them in the dog dish. He jumped down and gave Poncho a grumpy warning to stand clear.

Waving at the gang of teenagers, Deedee started the cooled auto and drove away. She had definitely misjudged the youth of this town. Maybe they would all be deaf in a few years, but they were all willing to help a stranded stranger—a damsel in distress. This new generation wasn't so bad. If she had been able to get pregnant when she had tried so many years ago, her child would now be a teenager.

Whimsically, she created that child in her mind. He was a boy with Daniel's black hair and chocolate-brown eyes. He was a straight A student and won honor roll every semester. Ambitious, he would want to go to Harvard but would settle for Yale or Cornell. With Daniel's brains and her creativity, he would want to be an astronaut or physicist.

No, he wouldn't have Daniel's black hair or brains. Daniel had been infertile. Why had he felt so strongly against insemination or adoption? She had wanted a child more than anything else in the world. Would he have loved one any less because his blood didn't flow in the child's veins?…because the little wiggler had not come from his loins? Her life would have been so different—so full of discovery and laughter.

Deedee admitted to herself that driving alone for such a long distance was rather like dying. Your life flashed before your eyes as the electrical poles and fence posts flashed across your windshield like blurring, marching soldiers, revealing every nuance of pleasure or disappointment. Yes—a lot like dying.

Nearer Sante Fe, the landscape gradually changed. The sunstruck ground showed larger patches of green on the gigantic feet of the Rockies. The blaring sun, that had sat on her lap all afternoon, moved behind the car and loomed in her rearview mirror. Short miles later it was shining in the passenger window. How could that be? She was traveling south. She pulled over to look at the map, assuming she had taken a wrong turn out of Sante Fe. Tracing the double rope of Interstate Twenty-Five, her jaw dropped.

"Look how far south it goes, Cisco."

As if he cared. Cisco looked at her perplexed and batted the paper out of her hand. Grabbing it and straightening its wrinkles, she looked at the lesser threads—the dotted lines. They cut diagonally out of Sante Fe. Then, she remembered Daniel's blunt warning every time she had traveled alone. "Stick to Interstate!" Knowing I-Twenty-Five would take her directly to Manitou Springs and then on to her destination, she shoved the map under the seat and decided not to venture onto the unknown, shorter route. Even in death Daniel guided (nagged?) her.

The map under the seat was a big mistake. Poncho continued, relentlessly, to scratch the paper into a cozy nest. Deedee decided to let him. The sun was sinking rapidly from the scorched sky, so maybe he would sleep.

Just before daylight disappeared, so did the mountains. She couldn't believe the flatlands that were leading her into Colorado. It seemed the Rockies were behind her. Was this the dust bowl?

The animals settled in the dark of the car after one more stop on the side of the road. Deedee scanned for a frequency on the radio since all of her pre-sets were lost by distance. Hearing a voice raised in anger and another soothing, she locked onto the talk program. She needed some sort of stimulation for the long drive. Sighing in relief at the sign that read "Colorado" she settled in to listen to the problems of her fellow human beings and a few miss-placed aliens. Through the weaving threads of human experience (not her own, of course) she might find the threads to weave her new novel. What had dried up the well of inspiration that had kept her an affluent writer? She wanted that wealth of words back again; was lost without them. Surely this move would help her.

The talk-show host croaked something crude and uncalled for at the tearful woman and hung up on her. Not knowing the reason for his anger, Deedee returned her concentration to the radio.

CHAPTER TWO

It was three-thirty a.m. when Deedee arrived at the small town of Green Mountain Falls. Everything seemed surrealistic, as if she had driven backward in time. The late hour intensified the weird sensation. Unbelievably, horse ties and wooden sidewalks lined the street. Had she mistakenly driven into a western theme park? No. The highway sign verified that she was on the right trail.

She pulled around the authentic western buildings and fished for the tape recorder in her glove compartment. Her realtor had sent a cassette tape with detailed, verbal directions to her cabin. Deedee pushed PLAY and drove back onto the highway.

Were those really hay bales stacked in the middle of downtown Green Mountain Falls? How wonderful.

Finding the sign that pointed to the falls, she turned and headed down the blacktop. Soon the woodsy cabins along the road thinned, and she came to a bridge. As she was crossing, she heard a rushing of water beneath her car.

"What in the world?"

Deedee found her cigarette-lighter spotlight and plugged it in. She needed to get out of the car, anyway, to stir wakefulness back into her bleary eyes. Shining the bright beam around her, she gasped. It was so fantastic with the light casting rainbows on the water as it rushed headlong under the bridge to cascade down the cliff, frothing into the stream far below.

All she had accomplished was to wake her animals. This being as good a place as any, Cisco was put on a leash. He began straining against the twanging leather and choked himself, coughing, anxious to explore the exciting new odors and altitude. The air hung heavy with mist, and Deedee caught a terrible chill, after the heat of the day, and was relieved to get back into the dry car.

When she found her turnoff, the stone-cragged road loomed straight up. She had to press the accelerator all the way to the floorboard before the little car would pull its burden up the road. After two more turns and another steep incline, she came to the dead-end turnaround that was described on the tape.

"End of the road, Guys." She didn't get much of a response. Having to probe around under the seat for several minutes, she finally found Poncho's furry warmth. He yawned and let her tuck his litheless body under her chin. Cisco, also, seemed to have lost all of his energy. She lifted his heavier weight against her side and trudged through the high grass to the wooden porch.

Deedee had left her purse in the car. Damn, she was so exhausted. Trying the door, she said, "What the heck? Who would need locks in this wilderness?" Not surprised that the door gave to her turn of the knob, she went into the pitch-black room.

Her leg brushed the couch beside the door. She didn't even search for a light switch. Nearly falling on the cushioned comfort, she snuggled her animals close and fell blissfully to sleep.

* * * * * * *

"Gooooooooooood God," Eric Broddery moaned when he glanced into the living room on his way to the john. His bare feet froze on the smooth, wooden floor—not from the cold—from immobility.

The morning sun had crept through the front window and caressed a golden, bare cheek. A goddess was sleeping on his couch. Her baggy shorts were scrunched up around her waist and exposed her glorious posterior.

Eric didn't think he could pull his eyes away from the vision until he saw her strawberry-blond hair catch fire with sunny radiance. He dropped his eyes to the luscious lashes resting against her freckled cheek. Wondering if the other cheeks were freckled as well, his eyes moved back down her length.

But a tan and brown head popped through her long hair and stared at him with beady black eyes. Then, a black fur ball rose from between her sprawled legs, and incessant yapping filled the room.

The lashes fluttered open. Startled, Deedee shot up, sending Cisco and Poncho both flying off-balance. She stared gape-jawed at the hairy man who stared back at her. His indrawn "Uhhhhhhhh" made her trace the trajectory of his sight. Her buttons had come undone during her restless sleep, and her cleavage was pressed toward him.

Deedee grabbed her blouse shut and sunk in her chest, trying to diminish her ample bosom.

He still stood staring. She gritted her teeth at the incongruity of the situation but couldn't prevent her eyes from getting larger as her light blue met his almost black. His hair hung past his shoulders and was in wild disarray. The light brown mixed with golden highlights contrasted dramatically with his very dark chest and leg hair. His beard was long and golden, brushing the massive expanse of his chest. Bulging, blue-striped boxers rode low on his diminutive waist and tapered hips. Deedee would swear to God if she had met this man in the woods she would have thought he was a grizzly bear. Absolutely Neanderthal.

"What are you doing in my house!" she stormed over Cisco's barks and growls.

"Your house?!" The voice roared. "Lady, I don't know who the hell you are, but YOU are the trespasser here!"

Looking around in confusion, Deedee saw that the hallway he stood in led to other rooms. There was a kitchen separated by a louvered screen. There was no sliding-glass door. A modern stove stared back at her in harvest gold from the kitchen, saying accusatively, "I am not a potbelly stove."

How could this happen? She had never been so embarrassed in all her life. Blood engorged the freckles on her face, painting them bright red. She stood up and lifted Cisco to quiet him. Poncho curled into a ball and went back to sleep, obliviously, in the puddle of warmth her bottom left on the couch cushion.

"How long have you been standing there?"

Eric was not about to tell her that he would have stood there absorbing her all day and for a lifetime if it hadn't been for her Poodle. "I have half a mind to call the police, lady. You break into MY home and expect me to answer YOUR QUESTIONS?! I deserve an explanation. Wait here."

Deedee was afraid not to obey the order. He continued on to the bathroom and left her standing in a puddle of self-loathing.

She straightened her clothing, buttoned and tucked her shirt, and ran her fingers through her disheveled hair. What was she doing—primping for a grizzly bear? She sat back down and Poncho barely escaped with his hide.

Hearing scraping from the front door, Cisco jumped down and lunged at the barrier, renewing the cacophony of his barking. The mountainous man came to the door and let a giant, hairy animal into the room. Deedee bolted for Cisco, but to no avail. The great beast's entire body was wagging as he touched noses to Cisco's in friendship. It was too, too ironic. Cisco usually bared teeth at every strange dog. Possibly, he saw the uselessness of that action…no…the danger of that action.

The huge dog reached Deedee in two strides and lathered her face in drooling welcome. She giggled and patted the massive, broad head. Realizing the awkward position she was in, she looked up at the tall man, her face once again somber. The acceptance from the large animal made her realize that she owed this man an apology for bursting into his home uninvited.

"I truly am very sorry. I thought this was the old Wilson place. It was very late and…"

"Damn tourists!" Eric interrupted her silky plea. "I watched them fixing that place up, and I knew it would mean trouble. You'll find an old stone stairway over there behind your car. The Wilson place is farther up the hill."

Deedee didn't like his tone, but she could hardly blame the man. How would she feel if the tables were turned? She scooped up her pets and had to squeeze between him and his animal to get out the door. At least he had donned his pants. Her silken voice changed to rasping ire. "Sorry! I won't bother you again," she said.

"Lady, I don't live out here for the company, and I don't entertain tourists."

With hair standing up on the back of her neck like a Halloween cat, Deedee looked up into his fuzzy face and felt his hot breath. Wanting more than anything to say something mean and nasty, she simply said, "Well, I bought the Wilson place, so get used to it." She trounced out the door and heard it slam behind her. "Well, I never!" she told Poncho and Cisco.

There was no road up the steep hill; only the steps the man had pointed out. Stopping at the car to retrieve her purse, she stuffed Poncho into its roomy interior and slung it over her shoulder. Letting Cisco run loose, she started up the stairs.

Deedee wasn't used to climbing the rugged country. By the time she reached the top of the hill, her knees were wobbling. She could barely see the stacked logs of the cabin through the trees. There was no porch; just an overhang covered the door. After fighting Poncho for the key, she turned the lock. SOME things were locked on this mountain. The man's house was probably locked by now.

Cisco ran ahead of her into the cool interior. Standing stock still, her eyes roamed the single room, and she groaned. A coiled spring pierced the couch in a cloud of cotton. The old tapestry upholstery was worn down to loose, bare threads. A rocking chair listed precariously by the potbelly stove. A greasy, black, wrought-iron square, on top of the potbelly, was the only place to cook her meals. Blond, wood patches streaked the open-beamed ceiling. A cot made from two-by-fours sat in a corner with a lumpy, feather mattress covered in dirty, striped ticking.

Groaning again, Deedee walked across the room to the only light source—the sliding glass door. It skreeled open and bounced in its track with gritty sounds.

The patio was an afterthought of a bad dream. New boards riddled old squeaky ones. The banister was new and looked safe, but she hopscotched from one new board to the next to reach it with relative safety.

The barkless timbers, that held it up, descended two stories down the mountain toward..."Oh my God," she groaned one more time. The grizzly bear was staring up at her with his hands on his hips, bare chested and poised like an ominous statue of pure testosterone.

His back door bit into the same incline, twenty yards from her support posts. Baring his teeth—was that a smile or a snarl?—he went back into his log cabin.

It took Deedee the rest of the day to move the contents of her trailer up the unending steps. She panted against the thin air and resorted to a sweater against the cool, mountain chill.

She caught several more glimpses of her neighbor, prancing around bare-chested. He must think her crazed to wear a sweater, but he had not come from one hundred-five degree temperatures.

After the work was done, she was famished. But she didn't have the energy to try the stairs to drive to a restaurant. She shuffled through boxes until she found a box of cereal and sat down on the sprung couch, popping sweet, dry food into her mouth.

Snatching a piece of paper from her purse, she began to write, not a novel but a list of what she would need to make this place survivable. She was not about to bare her bottom to the splintered seat in the outhouse for long, imagining all sorts of creatures lurking just beneath the abysmal hole ready to pounce on unprotected, tender flesh. She would retire with the sun rather than face the rickety building in the dark.

"Where the blinkety blank did the water go that they were supposed to hook up?" Setting the cereal box on the floor beside the couch, Deedee went out to search the periphery of the building. She found a faucet sticking up from the ground with a row of lumpy dirt clods running from it. "What did I expect—the kitchen sink? Why would I be so lucky?"

Slamming the door in defeat, she found Poncho had invaded the cereal box and was using it as a hiding place. Of course, the sweet treats were scattered all over the floor where Cisco was gobbling them up. There went her dinner.

Deedee had HAD it! Her suitcase was still in the car, and she knew for a fact she'd never be able to lug it the distance. She picked up her purse, picked up Poncho, called Cisco, and headed for the car. Tired, hungry, disgusted, cold, and shaking with anger, she got back in her car and drove back the way she had come. The empty trailer bounced in her wake on the rutted cow path.

"Motel or BUST!" she told her pets.

* * * * * * *

Eric watched her go. He hadn't stopped thinking about the woman all day and had stayed glued to the cabin just to watch her jaunty activity.

Failure at dealing with people had caused him to find this isolated retreat. He supposed he was a hermit. Everyone in town had learned to tolerate his mumbling responses to their queries.

"Nice day."

"Mmmmmmmmm."

"Hear we have a storm coming."

"Mmmmmmmmm."

"Do you want green beans or corn?"

"Mmmmmmmmm."

Big Dog was the only company he had kept in ten years. Today, he had rattled crude responses to the poor lady who had haplessly blundered into his home. He hadn't spoken more than two words to anyone for ten years.

Being a topnotch architect, Eric had been able to set his own rules. He handled everything through correspondence. All of his supplies arrived by mail carrier. Try as he might, he had never been able to find a way to buy groceries without seeing people. They wouldn't deliver out this far.

Turnabout being well accepted as fair play, Eric mounted the stone steps and came to the rickety door of her cabin. He wasn't surprised to find it unlocked. The lady had been pretty perturbed when she slammed her car door and stirred up a dust devil with her squealing tires.

Eric looked through the open boxes that were scattered across the cabin floor. He felt a little edgy, looking through her things, knowing it wasn't legal at the very least. Nor had been what she had done. If she had him arrested for breaking and entering, he would return the favor.

He found a box of books. Each had a lusty picture on its cover, and each read Deanna Drew DeVault as the author. So, she was a fan, or so Eric thought until he found her computer disks with identical titles. All of a sudden, his curiosity evaporated for her knickknacks. There was no way she would miss one of these disks, and he could easily replace it at a later date. He might be sneaky, but he was not a thief.

Looking behind him to see if the place was the way he had found it, he simply shrugged and left. He had found it a cluttered mess and was leaving it a mess.

Eric went to his office (spare bedroom) and, activating his computer, slipped in the disk. He padded his chair with pillows but spent the night in a great deal of discomfort, leaning into the screen. His discomfiture was mental as well as physical when her words stirred feelings in him long denied. He hadn't known he was still capable of yearning for female flesh, or that the longing still existed within him. Squirming from the sexual torture, he read long into the night.

Big Dog scratched for entrance after his nightly prowl, and Eric squinted against the daylight. Having read until four o'clock in the morning, he had slept very late. The little car hadn't returned. It saddened him, but he would take advantage of her absence. Pulling on his pants, he headed up the hill with her novel. It took him only moments to slip it back into the file and take another.

As he started down the steps, Eric was abashed when he saw the little car and trailer bouncing up the road with a truck riding high behind it. Backing away up the hill and saying a little prayer that she had not seen him, he walked back to the cabin and circled it. The slope was nearly straight down, but he had little choice. Skidding and bouncing on his bottom, he descended the rough incline.

The woman had him acting like a blundering idiot. He would never have dreamed of doing such a thing as slinking around like a common thief until she arrived. He had never been curious about other people or cared what they had behind their doors.

Eric slapped dirt from his bruised rump and torn hands, entered his back door, and made a beeline to the front door. He wanted to see what she was up to but felt like a peeping tom. To reprieve himself from the feeling, he went out onto his porch and rocked in his porch swing. When she looked his way, he waved nonchalantly.

Eric was starving. The sun said it was nearly noon and he hadn't eaten, nor showered, nor brushed his teeth. Yet, here he sat, watching men haul a heavy bureau, couch, and desk up the mountain. The lady must have been very busy during her absence, for another truck arrived carrying appliances, toilet, shower stall, lumber, and the kitchen sink complete with cabinets.

The lady was scurrying around, slavering over her new things. Eric didn't know what possessed him because he stood and shouted at her, "Don't like roughing it, huh?"

She glared at him, and her response was immediate."Where's your outhouse?!"

The laborers snickered at her quip and continued to unload.

One more truck arrived with logs, and Eric knew he was facing many more weeks of hammering.

* * * * * * *

Thank God the one room was so large. Once Deedee's cabinets, desk, and bureau were placed, the boxes seemed to unpack themselves. Deedee showed the carpenters where she wanted the cut for the bedroom door, right beside her new kitchen stove. They assured her the new windows in the original structure would be installed before the sun set. Her new bedroom/bathroom combo would have another sliding door accessing the soon-to-be-repaired balcony. The potbelly stove was already gone and would be replaced by a two-way fireplace between the living room and bedroom. Having no desire for air-conditioning on the cool mountain, she was, however, fantasizing about a roaring fire.

These men must have legs of iron. They didn't seem to tire from the myriad trips up the stone steps. The log truck did have a crane that spared them the hauling of logs, and the stack grew rapidly near the head of the hill.

Two weeks—two weeks they had promised for the extra thousand she had had to shell out. She hadn't expected the extra expense. The old saying, that you get what you pay for, held true, and she was paying and paying and paying.

She looked around the unpacked cabin. With the old stuff out, it already looked cozy and livable. For now, however, she had animals locked in a motel room, and she needed to tend them. There was nothing here worth stealing except her computer, and she would need that at the motel, anyway.

Deedee persuaded a husky man to carry it down to her car. She left the foreman a key but didn't see the need for one after the bedroom door was cut. Unhitching the little trailer and maneuvering it out of the way, she got back into her car for the trip back to Manitou. Her eyes moved to the shaded porch, betraying her. One more glimpse of the man before she left, but he wasn't there.

It was ludicrous for her to have to travel this distance to a motel, but it was just as well. She had gone into Colorado Springs this morning to make arrangements for her addition. The contractor had generously suggested a very reputable architect when Deedee had told him she wanted the best. She would pay another thousand to make sure her add-on didn't look added on.

Eric laughed out loud when the fax came in. He had already done the blueprints on the Wilson place when he had considered purchasing the cabin to keep neighbors out. It had occupied his time during a lull in business. It would take less than an hour to make some adjustments for the sliding door, patio, and fireplace.

Finally deciding he didn't want to bother with the rundown cabin that had been the hibernation headquarters of a mother bear and cubs during the winter, he had filed away his drawings. It would have been nice to have the extra office space, but the cost was exorbitant for the resulting product. This lady must be raking it in with her writing.

His own investments were growing astronomically and despite him, which only made good sense. He never touched his money, finding it distasteful and unnecessary. His broker and accountant handled everything, including the small amount the local grocer dunned him to survive.

Thank God for his fax. He sent the completed plans to the contractor and smiled at his deviltry—the easiest thou' he had ever made.

Big Dog plopped his over-large head on Eric's lap and whined for an ear rub. Ten years ago he had accepted the puppy as down payment for plans of a tobacco shop on an Indian reservation. Big Dog was an Indian dog of no particular breed though, surely, Irish Wolfhound must have been in his ancestry. He was getting old now. Ten years was a long life for a large dog. What would he do without the love and comradeship they shared? Several nights, recently, he had seen Big Dog lying on the porch throughout the night rather than running the hills he loved.

Eric thought of the woman and Big Dog's instant reaction to her and her animals. Big Dog held no qualms of doing what instinct drove him to do. But if Eric had done what instinct dictated, he would now be back in prison. He shuddered at the thought, but the shudder did not assuage the other sensations that wracked his body.

Knowing what red hair signified, he should have been forewarned of her hot responses. Was it the anticipation of that friction that compelled him to irritate her? Was it his longing for strong emotion from her? Any emotion?

She had looked so helpless with her little weasel and fluffy dog. He had wanted to wrap her up in his arms and protect her. But long habit and absolute isolation had guided his actions.

How must she have felt when she saw the horrid ruination she had purchased? He knew the price she had paid. Could he not, at least, try to turn the cabin into a comfortable home for her? But, wasn't that defeating his own purpose? He had moved up here to be alone. Would he, then, help her become an intruder? The helpless, citified woman couldn't help but be a nuisance.

The book—the words—the arousal—the novel had done something strange to him. He had pictured her as the heroine, regardless of the differing descriptions. The thoughts were, after all, coming from her mind. And, of course, he was the victim of her lust, her love.

If he worked with the contractor to oversee the construction, he could easily slip another disk from her file, and another, and another, and another. Eric wanted to know every single thought that permeated her brain.

He stood, dislodging Big Dog, and walked to the mirror in his bathroom. Looking into the revealing glass, he grabbed his beard and held it away from his chin. Eric would be sorry for its loss come winter. What was he thinking? This beard was as much a part of him as his work, cabin, dog. Maybe a little whack here and there—just a little trim.

* * * * * * *

The barber could not believe his eyes when he saw the old black jeep park in front of his establishment. Surely the hermit was going elsewhere. The barber stared agape when the door flew open and the bell tinkled.

The hermit's long stride brought him to the chair where he sat down in anticipation. Of what? What was the barber supposed to do? The man should go to a sheep shearer.

"A trim," the deep-timbred voice uttered, only causing further shock to the barber.

"The beard and the hair?"

"Mmmmmmmm."

"Do you want it short?"

"Unt uh."

"Just trimmed?"

"Mmmmmmmm."

Nearly shaking out of his skin, the barber proceeded to groom the monster. What if the hermit didn't like his haircut? Was he as dangerous as he looked? With great resolve, the barber took a firmer grip on his scissors and comb and started to whack away.

Pleased with the end result and praying the hermit was as well, the barber extended his hand for payment. A business card filled his palm that read—BILL TO JONES AND BREYER ASSOCIATES, and then the mailing address in Colorado Springs. The barber intended to claim a handsome tip for a job well done.

CHAPTER THREE

Deedee didn't know the strange man whom she saw talking to the foreman as he perused a blueprint. Freed of the added weight of length, Eric's hair laid in soft waves, barely brushing his shoulders. The blond beard was sculpted perfection and exposed his heart-shaped mouth. Dark chest hairs interlaced the placket of his white polo shirt, and the crisp pleats in his shorts pointed to the dark muscled legs and white sneakers. He turned, and the black eyes pierced her.

Another word to her foreman, and the man prowled past, like a panther stalking his prey, and took the stairs to return to his cabin.

Deedee couldn't believe this could be the same man. Astonishment led her to follow him with her wondering eyes until he disappeared behind his doorway, verifying the identity of the man as she had suspected.

Baffled, she watched his door for long moments before she went to the foreman to find out what was going on.

"What was HE doing here?" she asked.

"Just a nosy neighbor as far as I know, Ms DeVault." The answer seemed to satisfy her, so the crew foreman went about his business. In actuality, Eric Broddery was forcing him to secrecy, which he had willingly agreed to in order to have the architect on site.

Deedee watched in hypnotic trance as the carpenters shoveled the trench for the stem wall along the string lines. Her mind wandered from the automated movements.

What had wrought such a change in her neighbor? She had thought him handsome until she realized who he was. His wild hair was transformed into a head of hair even Amy would envy. His beard now gave his face character—but still foreboding—and framed his expressive mouth in its perfection. The knit shirt was stretched around his well-defined chest, teasing her thoughts to return to the hallway. The neatly-pleated, dark-blue shorts brought her memory avidly back to the boxers and the embarrassing, morning bulge that had drawn her eyes so blatantly.

She shivered, but not from cold, nor the bare chests of these workers. The grizzly bear had become a very human male of her species before her eyes, and desire scalded her to the fact that she was a very human female.

* * * * * * *

It had been too easy to gain access to her cabin. The foreman was anxious to have Eric there to read the blueprints. Even with the rush money the lady had shelled out, her contractor was over booked and had put his inexperienced crew on this job. With a little coddling and close supervision, the end result would not suffer.

The foreman was an experienced carpenter, but he had always relied on the contractor for specs. Eric wouldn't be needed again until they were ready to lay foundation molds. He would check their progress later in the day. But, for now…

Eric removed the stolen disk from under his waistband and popped it into the disk drive. Another hero, another plot, another victim of her imagination, he sat squirming, uncomfortably enraptured, while Big Dog wrapped around his feet.

* * * * * * *

Cisco spun in circles, and Poncho poked his head out from under the night stand when Deedee entered the motel room. She took a few quiet minutes to play, pat, and wrestle before going to her keyboard. She had a start for her book, finally, and wanted to get some notes down before they slipped elusively from her mind.

In one way, Colorado had been good for her. She spent little time dwelling on the past or pitying herself. There were far too many thoughts stirring her emotions at present.

Deedee was a little frightened at the rapidity of which her bank account was dwindling. The motel, construction, and architect were all expenses she had not planned on. Enormous amounts of money had been spent on furnishings and appliances. Thank God the addition's cost included the plumbing and fireplace.

She would have to go ahead and transfer her mail and establish a local bank account with her royalty checks. There was nothing left from the insurance policy, and Daniel had always managed to spend everything he made on extravagances—anything and everything that would impress other people. She could sell his Mercedes. She could sell his diamonds, but they were locked away in a safe deposit box in Tucson. If Deedee was frugal, she should be able to manage on income.

Manage on income. Memories stirred of the struggles Daniel and she had gone through right after she got out of school. He had just graduated from Arizona State but had three more years of law. The loans were incredible, and she had had to work full time to make ends meet. The few short stories that she had been able to write and sell had kept her love of writing fresh.

Her college education had to wait until Daniel was a practicing lawyer. Feeling a little like a second fiddle, she had finally graduated. There were no trumpets—or fiddles. Many of her credits had been obtained through night courses. Deedee graduated mid-term and, so, lost all of the ceremonious, marvelous hoopla that accompanied graduation. Instead of celebration, she simply received relief from Daniel that he no longer had to endure her long, study hours. But that didn't change. She spent them writing.

Casting painful memories aside, Deedee thought about the bedroom door the carpenters would hang tomorrow. She could move back in. The bedroom furniture crowded the single room, right now, but she couldn't afford the high cost of a motel and would just have to tolerate the squeeze for a few weeks. The plumber would arrive in the morning to bring civilization back into her life by hooking up her kitchen sink.

The cost of a septic system was unbelievable. The contractor had suggested that tying into the neighbor's would be more practical, but she had quelled that proposition on the spot. The less she had to do with the irate man, the better.

Deedee could understand the man's defensiveness concerning tourists. It seemed as if every shop, every attraction, every park were keyed to draw them. She had even seen a sign advertising gold digging or "panning" was the word they used. Incredible! Did people really still do that? What drew all of these people? She had always believed Colorado was for skiing. There was no snow on those slopes on this pleasant July day, and yet, the motels were packed and cars swarmed through the downtown area. Deedee had even seen horseback riders and Indians in full headdress on the streets of Manitou Springs, regressing her once again to the days of the Old West.

Were all of these things the reasons that her neighbor felt so comfortable with his uncivilized appearance? It was apparent he could look very professional if he half tried. She had thought he was her architect when she saw him early this morning. Deedee chuckled at the ridiculous thought.

He looked so masculine and clean. Odd, she had never used the word "clean" as a description for a man before, even in her novels. Had she thought him dirty because of his unsightly hair and unkempt appearance on the morning they had so misfortunately met? She had felt an urge to take her Poodle clippers to his motley head. Another memory disturbed her. She thought of Daniel's complete lack of hair on top of his head and his little joke of rubbing all of it off on the headboard. Did that correlate somehow?

Daniel had been tall compared to her, but the neighbor's height dwarfed him with his burly stature. Daniel had been soft spoken, but her neighbor's voice roared with a rough timbre like pine trees grating against each other in a storm. Daniel's chest had been smooth and hairless when she caressed it; the neighbor's was a hairy weed garden of bristling, dark fur.

What was she doing? Why was she comparing them like merchandise in a mall? It was unthinkable. Deedee shook her limbs to vibrate the thoughts from her brain.

She keyed in her new file name. It was a beginning. "Tall Timbre" she read. Looking at the anomalous spelling, she moved her cursor over then, shrugging, left the spelling alone. It suited.

After a restless sleep, Deedee packed up her remaining belongings from the motel room. The morning air was cool and misty, and she envisioned a blazing fire. She went back into the room to search for Poncho while Cisco yipped and jittered in the car. Finally finding Poncho under her crumpled covers, she whisked him out to the car.

When she arrived at Green Mountain Falls, a trail ride was getting underway. She was surprised at the ages of some of the young children who rode by themselves. One couldn't have been out of diapers more than a year. Frightening! But, who was she to judge? She had no experience in rearing young. Only the unknown could truly be feared, and, to her, children were the unknown.

Deedee suddenly realized that she was yet young enough to bear a child. A broad grin split her lightbulb face, and several of the riders grinned and waved. Jubilant at the brilliant truth, she grinned ever broader and waved at the happy tourists and their children. CHILDREN! She was only thirty-four, and God had seen fit to make her fertile. Why not?

The idea consumed her throughout the long drive to the cabin, and she still wore a happy smile when she topped the stone stairs and stared into the black eyes once again. Cisco was running circles at his feet, relishing his renewed freedom, and the gargantuan dog galumphed across and landed a giant paw against Cisco's backside, sending him flying. Recovering, Cisco ran in nipping at giant heels. He circled barking. There were no growls. They both ran into the heavy woods to play. The growls were in Deedee's closed mouth. Her neighbor didn't greet her. He mumbled something incomprehensible and walked past her.

Had Deedee seen a corner of his mouth quirk upward? He had looked so…so…so like a man. Very poetic, Deedee. Is that the best you can do? He's a "clean" "man". How profound. She hit her head, trying to dislodge some of the mud clogging her gray matter, shrugged, and continued toward her cabin.

The bedroom door was hung, but there was no hardware on the door. Locating the foreman, she asked him, "Will the handles be put on before tonight?"

"I'm sorry, Ms DeVault. The drop latches are replicated, and we had to order them. They won't be in until some time next week."

"How will I lock my house?!"

"I don't know. We'll try to rig something temporary."

Deedee, dragging the foreman behind her, went into her living room and looked around. If the door only opened inward, she could block it with a knife or chair. The heavy bureau caught her eye. "Can you scoot this up against it?" She pointed to the heavy piece of furniture that should block the entire opening.

"Certainly. That will work fine until we get the bedroom framed in. We'll move it before we leave."

"Thank you. That would be a relief. You can call me Deedee, by the way. What's your name? We're going to be sharing close quarters for a while; we might as well be on a first name basis."

"Yeeees."

The foreman visibly brightened, giving Deedee second thoughts about first names.

"Call me Greg—Greg Thompson, Ms…a…Deedee."

He shook hands as if they were meeting for the first time. Deedee felt great relief when he relinquished her hand from his callused one. She could swear she felt a splinter prick her palm and looked at her hand briefly.

"Well, Greg," it would be Greg, reminding Deedee of Amy's beaus, "could I impose on you to run a light to my outhouse? I would be glad to pay the extra. It looks as if it will be several days before I have facilities here."

"I'd be happy to oblige, free of charge. My daddy always taught me that a favor is returned ten fold. There's a hardware store in town. I recommend you go there yourself. Just tell them you need a one-hundred-foot, outdoor extension cord and a trouble light. We'll do the rest when you return. I have strict orders to keep working come hell or high water, if you get my drift. The man who carried your computer, the other day, really got a railing from the contractor."

Oh great. Her computer once again required carrying, uphill instead of down. She decided to wait until these men went home to do the task, not wanting to be the cause of another "railing". Who had squealed on the poor, helpful man who had assisted a lady in distress?

On no, Cisco was no where in sight. She couldn't leave him here while she drove to the hardware store. Poncho was still lying quietly in her purse. She began to call Cisco. "Here Cisco. Come on boy. Cisco! He-e-e-ere Ci-i-isco!" She heard a shrill whistle but didn't know from whence it came.

The hairy, huge dog came lumbering out of the forest with a bouncing, black ball in his wake.

Relieved, Deedee scooped Cisco up while his friend made his way ungracefully down the stairs.

She went back to her car, her eyes flying, like swallows to Capistrano, to the porch swing—the empty porch swing.

* * * * * * *

Eric stood behind the reflective glass—the sun mirroring its surface in the morning light—filling his eyes with her. He knew she couldn't return his gaze. She wore a light blue sweatsuit, bagging on her lean frame. He knew what lay beneath the deceiving, thick fabric.

So unlike his wife, who had been heavy-boned and as rugged as he, this woman was delicate, feminine, alluring, mysterious. Her thoughts were becoming intertwined with his own as he read her vivid romances. Eric supposed he was a pervert as well as a hermit, having already kissed that golden rump in his mind, nestled his nose in the depth of her cleavage. The sprawled legs had sprawled for his benefit, and he was there between the graceful limbs in the stead of her Poodle. He had kissed the fluttering lashes open, and it was him running fingers through her hair in the stead of her weasel—the morning sun spotlighting and caressing the god and goddess in their rapture.

Eric moaned. It had been long years since such thoughts plagued him. His past had bludgeoned sex from his brain and body as certainly as the mountains played hide-and-go-seek with the sun.

How could they have believed him capable of such an atrocity? He had never harmed another living creature in his life. To avoid a squirrel, he would nearly run his jeep off of a cliff. My God, how could they have thought it was him?

No one had dared approach him in prison. The pretty boys had drooled and cooed, but he ignored them. The toughs looked the other way when he passed unspeaking, isolated, and alone through the years and bars. No, sex could not be thought of. To do so would have meant the end of his sanity. Celibacy was his defense against the inhuman prosecution, the groaning zombies in prison seeking release in one way or another, the curious stares of his ex-friends after exoneration. Celibacy had contained the delicate flower of his sanity like the Mother held the mighty pine.

Now, that flower was withering in the bright July radiance of the woman. What would he call her? Neither her first name nor her middle name suited her. He couldn't bring himself to call her Deanna or Drew. Perhaps "Helen" of Troy or "Venus" Goddess of Love. Yes, Venus. She was his Venus and just as cold and inaccessible.

Eric went back up the hill to check the foundation plumbing and the stem wall molding. The portable cement mixers would be hoisted to the top of the hill tomorrow, but he wouldn't be present to hear the grumblings of the men, spoiled by premix. The men began digging the septic hole. Eric felt a tug of sympathy. No back hoe would scoop the ground, no crane would lift the cross beams and trusses for the roof. They were reduced to the methods of their ancestors. Eric was surprised they hadn't made the woman cut a drive in the hill. If he had been the contractor, he would have insisted on it or refused the incredible task and deadline.

Walking the periphery of the new room, Eric pointed out a listing frame. He pulled a tiny level out of his pocket and let it rest on several locations. The plumbing didn't require his inspection after all. He knew the old plumber well. He was half Indian, which had probably prompted the perfection of his work. Eric would not insult the man by inspection. He simply nodded a greeting, words unnecessary to either of them due to common respect.

Being a man of few words, communicating most of his instructions by pointing or demonstrating, Eric was startled at the outburst of the foreman.

"My name's Greg. Of course, I already know your name. Deedee still doesn't know, though. Why the big secret? You got something going with her?"

Deedee…Deedee…Deedee, the name roiled in his mind, obliterating the question that hung suspended in the air anticipating an answer. Yes, Deedee suited her—like the start of a song or a bouncing ball. Deedee delightful. "Huh?"

"I said, 'What's the big secret?'"

"Mmmmmmm."

* * * * * *

The room progressed steadily while Deedee steadily lost her mind. She had turned the stereo up full blast against the grating mechanics of the cement mixers. No sooner had she fallen into the lovely quiet of the night, when she was blasted back to wakefulness by nails being wrenched from boards and boards clanking together in stacks. Then, the nail guns hammered and zipped. A few more hours of midnight sleep and…"My God, is that a chain saw?" Bolting from her bed, she stared unbelieving out the window on the morning of the third day.

Four men carried a log toward her, chipped out and pre-drilled for…"My God, are those railroad spikes? No. They're bigger." Sledge hammers bammed; she pulled on her pants. The chain saws burred; she pulled on her shirt. Logs whammed together; she escaped through the door and took to the hills. Extreme hunger was the only thing that would drive her back to the ear-splitting racket.

She climbed through the maze of trees. Cisco showed her the way, idling in overdrive for her slower pace. The sounds of construction became muffled by the thick growth, an echo ringing in her ears. She heard a bubbling chortle and followed the sound, a more pleasant one than what she had endured.

Poor Poncho, he must be frightened out of his wits. She hadn't taken the time to discover his sleeping place, always a new one every night—like Amy. Deedee giggled.

The trunks began to thicken in width, their numbers thin. Feeling insignificant under their towering nobility, she felt like a man on the moon—an intruder in an alien place—a place to be seen from afar but left untouched.

The brazen little bonsai caught her eye. How could it be here? Natural, glorious, pristine, it seemed to rebel against the mighty forest, holding more power in its tiny limbs and knobby knees than all of the giants combined.

Deedee dropped down beside it in worship of the improbability of it. This tiny tree pulled strings inside her. It was like her. Overpowered by the world, it sat alone but inspired and awed in its solitude. Like her, it was rooted, satisfied with its small spot on Earth. Or was that like her? Hadn't she uprooted herself and moved to a very strange spot indeed?

It didn't belong in a pot—a prisoner of the person who potted it. This was its place and here it would stay. Those who wished to worship would have to come to its temple— its sanctuary. It was ageless. Deedee knew if she severed the trunk, she could count its age, destroy it to sate her curiosity. But it wouldn't be necessary. The tree said, with emphasis on every miniature needle, that it was far older than she and deserved her respect.

Cisco lifted his leg and peed on the little tree before she could stop him. She jolted upward, barely clear of the offending stream herself. Oh well, nature took care of her own. No harm would come from his action, only from her own thoughts of a pot and a very valuable treasure lying at her feet. She scoffed at the people who panned for gold and walked right by this precious gem, unaware of its value.

Deedee moved on. Her legs, unaccustomed to the uphill climb, began to tire. The stone stairs had strengthened her somewhat. She wouldn't have been able to go this far when she first arrived. Why had she let her muscle tone become so flaccid? Hers were muscles of the mind. She imagined that she burned more calories writing than she did, now, by walking. It was certainly more work, to think, and write, and wrack her brain.

The sounds of water caught her ear again. Thank heavens, the sound seemed to be coming from downhill. Deedee headed in the proper direction to find the stream.

"How lovely." Chips of glitter—gold?—glinted under the sparkling water, and the sun danced on the ripples. The trees seemed to afford this brook its space and stood aside, clearing a path through the forest for its passage. Deedee followed.

Nature called, from the sounds of water, and she took care of it naturally. She had never felt so alive in her life. How could that be? How could she feel so alive in this quiet, lonely, foreign place?

Hearing the big dog howl a plaintive plea, she wondered where Eric was. Frantically looking behind her, she then scolded herself for such thoughts. What did she think he was—a stalker? If he was there, he had once again gotten an eyeful of her bared posterior. Deedee would have to be a little more careful in the future.

What would/could she do if he jumped from behind a tree and tried to rape her? Scream, of course, but who would hear her over the horrendous noise of her construction? Did she think the mountain man capable of such an act? She didn't have that answer. He was so unreachably mysterious. How could she get beneath that cold veneer?

Surprised by her musings, she wondered why she dwelled on him so often. Something about him intrigued her. Maybe he was simply a mystery unsolved.

Further down the stream, the ringing sledges returned to reverberate in her eardrums. She felt like a filthy criminal, desecrating this wonderful world of peace with the riot of sound that she had demanded. She would count the days. It had now been only five since the work began, three of them spent on this mountain.

Hunger drove her home.

CHAPTER FOUR

Big Dog scraped the door with his nails, and Eric answered. Eric wasn't about to let him or the little black dog, beside him, enter. The stench nearly knocked him from his feet. Eric went to get a rope and secured Big Dog to the porch rail. He looped another around the Poodle's neck and fairly dragged him up the stone steps.

Fighting and reluctant to go home, the Poodle slipped the loop and ran back to Big Dog, protesting for his protection. Eric started all over with a tighter loop.

Deedee answered the banging door. The only way she knew someone was knocking, instead of hammering, was by the vibration of the boards on the old door.

When she opened it, the odor of death smacked her in the nostrils. "What have you done to my dog?!!" she accused in shock.

"You don't know much about dogs, do you?"

"What? Answer me! What happened?!"

"Lady, this is sweet perfume to him. He's been rolling on a dead animal. Big Dog did the same. I'll help you clean him up if you'll help me. Believe me, I'll get the better bargain."

She didn't know what to make of his cordial proposition. He seemed sincere. He had felt enough compassion for Cisco to bring him to her. Could there be a friendship, or more, lurking behind this excuse to be with her? Anxious to be free of the tension that clouded their every meeting, she would take him up on his offer.

Deedee didn't even want to touch Cisco. She pointed to the kitchen sink, and Eric lifted the little Poodle—using two fingers and his thumbs—to the bright new enamel. He put down the drain plug and ran lukewarm water into the bowl.

Four arms battled for faucet, soap, cups, and drain plug, faucets and cups again, then towels. Their hips bumped together and they laughed at Cisco's sad predicament and their own. Soon the whole room smelled just like Cisco had, and Cisco smelled spring fresh.

With Cisco comfortably ensconced on the couch in a big, fluffy towel, Eric slipped a disk into its file and removed another while Deedee rubbed the Poodle fuzz briskly. Once the book was secured under his waistband, his solid stomach ridges holding it flat, Eric grabbed Deedee's hand and pulled her out the door.

"A deal is a deal," he stated, dragging her toward his cabin. "Wait here. I'll get what we need." Eric removed the disk and hid it beneath a newspaper before he went to his bathroom to get shampoo and towels. A disk might stay dry during a Poodle bath but not a Big Dog bath.

Eric placed the shampoo and towels on the rail and disappeared around the side of the house. He came back carrying a spewing hose, and Big Dog writhed, and squirmed, and backed up the porch rail in his frenzy to escape.

"Stand behind him and straddle his rump," Eric calmly instructed. "Clamp him tight between your thighs. Thank God you're wearing shorts, for a change, because you're going to get wet."

Deedee stared at him with her mouth open, and Eric grinned. The ordeal began. Fur flew. It was raining water from every direction. Big Dog shook off every few minutes, and Deedee's teeth rattled in unison. Deedee's shirt plastered to her skin, and she bent over, holding onto Big Dog's neck to gap the shirt away from her breasts. The result was red hair plastered to her face and soap spitting up into her eyes from Big Dog's tremors. Water and soap were sluicing down her legs and into her tennis shoes.

She glared at the mountain man, wondering why he didn't see her peril, and she guffawed at his own dripping locks and clinging clothes. He was alternating which eye to look through, and his eyes looked like blinking light shutters on a ship. Too bad, she didn't know Morse code.

Finally, Eric stood back and shot a blasting, rinsing spray. "Stand back!" he shouted.

Big Dog turned into a blur of fluffing fur and flying water. Any particular dry spot that had existed on Deedee's body became instantly doused. They both took towels to him—already wet towels—and squeezed water from his feet and tail. Deedee lifted a flopping, heavy ear and swathed it out.

Exhausted, elbows trembling, Deedee threw the towel over the rail. "Whew, I'm glad that's over."

"Sorry, we're not done yet."

"What do you mean?"

"We have to find the dead animal. Both of these dogs will go right back and redo themselves with perfume."

Deedee groaned at the aspect. "I don't understand. How could we find it? There's too much country to cover. It would take weeks. Can't we just keep them tied up?"

Deedee saw a change come over the man's happy face. A grim shade was drawn, turning day into gloomiest night. She had said something to cause this change. Or was it her reluctance to obey him that turned him into a remote statue? She had heard there were men who would accept nothing less than immediate action to their orders. Was he one of them? She didn't press him but stood her ground. Slowly, his attention came back to her, but the joy was gone from his mouth and eyes.

Eric rumbled, "I will NOT tie my dog!"

"But he's tied now," Deedee retorted.

The angry man took the rope from the rail and led the wet dog into his house, leaving Deedee, once again, standing in a puddle of self-loathing and total confusion.

* * * * * * *

Eric kicked the door to the john. He grabbed his bruised toe and jumped on one leg down the hallway, stringing four letter expletives together while Big Dog whined and looked at him through cocked eyes. "Damn it!" Why had he done that? Why had he let his own failures ride on someone else's shoulders? It wasn't Deedee's fault that he dreaded the thought of being locked up. "For Christ's sake, she was talking about my dog, not me!"

"I'm so STUPID! An idiot! An imbecile! I didn't even have the balls to call her by name."

Things had been going so great. They were having fun, and laughing, and wrestling with Big Dog. He could see her nipples, twisted into hard fruit from the cold water. The flowers on her panties promised a garden of delight beneath her white shorts. He had wanted to kiss the drops streaming from her nose and lap the water collecting on her lips. He had wanted to count every freckle on her body and kiss each one so she would know how precious they were to him.

He moaned and limped to the coffee table. Removing the disk from beneath the newspaper, he carried it to his office. He could have her this way. He would be the one lying in her arms or mounting her body in hardened readiness. He would have a different name, a different job, a different home, but what mattered to him would be the same. He would make love to the woman he loved…in his dreams.

* * * * * *

When the crew left for the dinner hour, Deedee heard it. Bees? No. Flies. Of course, she could find a dead animal in the woods. The smell would direct her. The flies would direct her. She snatched up the small trowel she kept with her kitchen utensils and headed out the door, turning her head to find the sound.

Heading into the high country, Deedee knew she would not have to go far. The odor was pungent, and the buzzing blared. It was, when she found it, or had been, a chipmunk. She poked at the remainder of stripes along its back, incredulous that such a small creature could create such a horrid stench on the massive Big Dog. The poking discouraged the flies temporarily, so she began to dig the hole.

The ground was extremely resilient—hard packed and solid with no grass to cut it. Deedee chipped away at the stone-like surface and, eventually, a tiny clod popped up. Being fractionally upwind from the death gases wasn't helping. She didn't know how much longer she could handle it. A large shovel bit the dirt beside her spade, and two giant boots drove it into the earth.

Turning her head, Deedee looked up the length of him. She felt awed as her eyes traveled up his body. He didn't speak. He didn't meet her eyes. He went on digging robotically. The hole was soon ample, and she used the stick to scoot the decaying mass into it. Ground began to cover it.

She stood and faced him. The black eyes were vague. Gone was the anger, but the happiness was also gone. He didn't speak but looked into her eyes for long minutes. Like a fidgety animal, Deedee pulled her eyes away.

"Thanks," she said.

"Mmmmmmmm."

Deedee gathered her small tool and started back toward her cabin. The sounds of construction had returned to break the quiet of the forest.

* * * * * * *

Eric stood and watched her until he could no longer see her clearly. Her walk was brisk yet sensual. He could see the slight twitch in her hips, indicating her anger. Did she know what her body was saying? Possibly. She must know he was watching her. After she was out of sight, Eric started back to his cabin. He had a book to read. It was just getting to the juicy part.

Before he lost himself in the rolling screen, he sent a fax to Jones and Breyer requesting five hundred cash be transferred to the local bank. Changing his mind, he reneged the order. Eric would go into the Springs tomorrow. He desperately needed new clothes.

Dreading the thought of shopping far more than the simple act of burying the dead animal or the Big Dog bath, he, nonetheless, had a greater purpose in mind. The result might be worth the painful effort.

* * * * * * *

Deedee sat on her couch, petting and snuggling her animals. Her thoughts were riveted to the mysterious man. Why was she so drawn to him? His heart was so cold. Had it just been too long since she had had a man—any man? No. There were bare-chested men aplenty on her hilltop. She could wiggle any one of them into the woods on a whim.

It wasn't her overheated passion that drove her. Something had pulsed and passed between them when his hand had engulfed hers and dragged her down the stairs. Her heart had fluttered out of control, thinking of a tryst in his cabin, unknowing of the grueling task in store for her. But she had enjoyed every minute of the stinky bath.

This man hadn't realized that wet clothing revealed every outline of his physique to her longing eyes. He had not attempted to hide it, as had she. He may as well have been nude when he stood and used the hose to rinse the beast. A shiver ran down Deedee from the memory.

Big Dog—what a name for the massive animal. Was it a lazy name from a lazy mind, or was it something so original she would never encounter it again? The words used in this new world were not very inspiring: clean, man, big, dog. But the mystery of it all was. Determined to search for the root of this towering timber, she pulled her desk chair out onto her patio slats and sat near the banister. The sun had set; the workers had gone. She stared toward the unlighted windows and feared he wasn't home.

There! She saw a flicker on a face. Of what? Her eyes adjusted to the dark night, and slowly the image became more clear. She felt like a spy, certainly a nosy neighbor herself, but she couldn't help what she saw from her balcony. He could pull the drapes if he wanted privacy, and how many times had he watched her through his windows?

It was a computer screen that glowed. His fingers were idle on the keys. His hand braced up his hairy chin as he seemed to study something. Amazed at the computer, amazed he could read, amazed at his studious behavior, Deedee slipped back into her cabin.

Morning would bring the dawn—the dawn of discovery as she searched and researched this man. She didn't even know his name. She made up a name, sitting before her screen. Her fingers flashed on the keys. Deedee would write the torrid love scene that boggled her brain. She would fill in around it later. Amy's words came back to paralyze her—"DO, DO, DO, instead of WRITE!"

She hadn't thought of Daniel for a very long time. Had her past life evaporated in the new sensations of this mountain man? Surely, it was the construction that occupied her mind, the shopping for new furnishings, the problems and pounding. Sixteen years of marriage could not slip away so easily. But, Daniel did slip away, once again, as her words filled the screen.

* * * * * * *

Eric watched the little car pull away shortly after the hammering started. It was eight o'clock in the morning, but he didn't judge time by a clock. The morning sun sent dust motes dancing across his couch where her shapely bottom had been. It was time to start the day, always with the memory of her filling his mind. He had many things to do, many errands to run—abnormal behavior for the hermit pervert.

First, he would take the opportunity of her absence to return the disk and retrieve another. Eric entered the cabin on the pretext of checking the doorframe. The desk chair was pushed back from her desk. Had she been working? Eric crossed the room and activated her computer. A file name drew his interest—Tall Timbre. He brought it up and scanned the words quickly. Shocked, he fell in her chair and stared at the screen intently.

"Penelope." He said her name like the gentle strains of a calliope. Roger brought his large, soft hands up to circumvent her full breasts and took possession of them with gentle pressure. Penelope moaned as his blond beard cushioned his teasing tongue. Her body arched upward toward him, drawn by the scent of pine and animal musk. She thrust her being into the hardness of him, seeking relief from the tremors that shook her…

Eric heard footsteps on the small slab of a porch. He switched off the computer and hurried toward the door, shaken by the close call. He noticed the rise in his pants. "Damn!" Kneeling quickly in front of the kitchen sink, he ripped the cabinet open.

"I heard a rattle under here the other day. Thought I'd better check the pipes," Eric said to the unknown person who entered.

The old Indian stared at him when he turned, amazed at the string of words that had come from the hermit's mouth.

Eric looked embarrassed. He picked up a can of cleanser. "Just a can hitting the pipes," he rattled.

"Nothing wrong with the pipes, Mr. Broddery?"

"No, no, of course not!"

The plumber grumbled and set down his tools, and Eric made a fast escape. "Dumb," he had forgotten to pick up another disk, but the page on her screen had been worth the oversight. It was apparent to him that she thought about him, at least occasionally, in the same way he thought about her.

He brushed his blond beard, with his hand, and imagined it pressed against her breast, his tongue teasing her nipples into arousal.

With a strange sound coming from his mouth, he got into his jeep for the trip to Colorado Springs. Big Dog howled from inside the house, insensate at the imprisonment. Eric cringed and revved the engine to life.

* * * * * * *

Deedee procured no information whatsoever from the grocery store. No one in this town seemed to know the man's name. Several shocked expressions had blurted, "The hermit?"

This was going to be harder than she imagined. Every question she asked was met with shrugs or blunt consternation.

Deedee went into the barbershop, and the men there glared at her as if she had broken some ancient taboo. The barber broke into a grin when she described the mountain man.

"Yeah, he was in here a few days ago for a haircut and trim. It nearly floored me to see him walk through the door. I never thought I'd see such a thing in my lifetime."

"Do you know his name?"

"No. Hey, are you that writer who moved into the old Wilson place?"

She nodded.

"No wonder you're so damn interested. It must be pretty scary living a hand's throw from that man. He scares me out of my pants just to look at him. At least, he went out of here a little less hairy than he came in."

"Please, do you know anyone who might know him? I'm desperate. I'm at the end of my rope."

The barber felt sorry for the lovely lady in her high heels and business suit. She looked out of her element in Green Mountain. He went to his register and fished under the tray. A white card came out between his fingers, and he brought it to her.

"This is all I got. You can't have it; I need it for billing."

Deedee smiled and rummaged through her purse for something to write on. She handed the card back to the frisky looking barber and said, "Oh, thank you. Thank you so much. You're a life saver."

"I hope you don't mean that literally, lady," he hollered as she headed out the door. The barber crossed his arms and boasted out his chest, looking smugly at the men around him.

Deedee entered Jones and Breyer very hopeful that, at last, she would get some answers. She was dressed to impress. Her slim pink business suit was tailored to her figure with perfection. Casual clothing would not exude the answers she was determined to hear.

The secretary was a guard dog, "Do you have an appointment? Mr. Jones and Mr. Breyer have a very full schedule."

"No, I don't have an appointment. I only need a moment of their time. Either associate will do. Please, this is very important," Deedee begged.

"I'll see if Mr. Breyer is free."

The woman disappeared behind a door. A man came out and shook Deedee's hand. "How can I be of assistance Ms...a..."

"DeVault," she filled in. "I'm trying to find out a little something about my neighbor, and I understand he's one of your clients."

"Come into my office," he stated frankly.

Before she had even seated herself, Mr. Breyer began to lecture. "Ms DeVault, I hold my client's affairs in strictest confidentiality. Your request is somewhat out of line."

"No. You don't understand. I'm not, in the least, interested in his financial affairs. I simply want to find out a man's name. He lives next to me near Green Mountain Falls. The town's people call him a hermit. Please, just a name and an occupation." Her curiosity was escalating. "The man is frightening, and he's my neighbor. Consider me a damsel in distress—much distress."

Deedee eyeballed him to grade his expression and her impression on him. She saw an F for failure and continued her spiel. "I'm writing a new romance novel with this mysterious man as the key character. All I'm asking is for simple research information. Surely, his name and occupation would not strain your business relations. I would ask him myself if I had the courage. He IS formidable." Deedee offered the man a terrified pout and won an A+.

"All right, all right." At this point he would do anything just to get rid of the pleading female, but he had finally heard a spark of truth in her plea. "Do you have his address?"

Deedee blurted the information, and Mr. Breyer cross referenced it on his screen.

"Oh, of course, the man is Eric Broddery, a fine architect. I've never met him personally, but soon will. Quite a coincidence, he has an appointment at nine-thirty."

Quickly, Deedee looked at her watch. Five minutes! Her heart sank. She had to get out of here, NOW! She shook Mr. Breyer's hand. "Thanks. Thanks ever so…"

The door opened, and Eric Broddery entered. "Damn it," she muttered under her breath, "why did the guard dog let HIM slip by so easily?"

"Well, thanks again Mr. Breyer. I'll take that under advisement." She winked conspiratorially and slithered past the mountain man, looking shocked at his presence.

"What? Hello neighbor. You should have told me about this fine establishment. I had to discover it on my own." She smiled imperceptibly and fled.

"What was SHE doing here?" the animal growled.

Mr. Breyer shrugged and introduced himself, very shaken.

Deedee went to see her contractor. He wasn't there. She was given directions to the building site where she could find him. She was pissed off.

Trudging over the rough ground, high heels wobbling and threatening to break her ankles, she scowled at the wolf whistles of the working carpenters. Finding the man, she approached him with nostrils flared.

"For God's sake, why didn't you tell me my architect lived right next door?!" she bellowed.

Taken aback, he stuttered, "M-m-ms DeVault, I d-don't know what you're talking about. Do you mean that Eric Broddery is your neighbor?"

"Yes, damn it, and I had to go snooping around like a hound dog to find that out. No wonder he's been prowling around my construction. It's his design! How could you do this to me?!"

"Now, hold on, Lady. I didn't have any idea Mr. Broddery lived close to you. All I have is a fax number. He could live on the moon for all I know."

Deedee was shaking. Her vehemence for this man melted. She no longer had a target for her embarrassment and anger. She broke down in wails of tears. Hating herself for her weakness—the only remaining release for her pent up ire—she stalked away, muttering incomprehensible apologies.

Sitting in her car, she tried to recoup some of her composure. What had gotten into her? She rarely went on such tirades. Why would she be so upset by the little trick this Eric Broddery had played? No wonder he wouldn't tell her his name. One thousand dollars of her money now lined his wallet. She had thought he was poor. "Ha!" The clothes he wore were usually ragged and torn. The jeep he drove was so old she wouldn't even attempt to name the year. He had fooled her so completely.

That was where her rage lived. That was where her tears had come from. She was a DUPE and had wailed her indignation as the realization pervaded her brain.

The poor contractor. She had lashed out at a man who was completely innocent of the scam. Getting back out of her car, taking her shoes off, and ruining her hosiery, she trooped back over to the sulking man.

She cooed her heartfelt apologies, a bit more sincerely, until a smile returned to his face, and then praised him for the rapid progress on her house. He promised to come out to inspect "the situation".

Deedee headed home. Insane thoughts battled in her mind. Murderous thoughts fought with need and desire. There was one thing she could NOT deny. This man was manipulating her in ways she had not been aware of. He was reclusive and secretive. Scary? No, she was not afraid of him. She was afraid of herself.

Entering her house, she took the onslaught of her pets and exhaled her in-held breath. Thank God for Poncho and Cisco. They were an anchor on the restless sea she rode.

She went to her computer to enter the ideas she had formulated on the highway. It was a wonder she had come up with anything after the turmoil that had set her off. Deedee picked up the disk that lay by her keyboard. She turned it over and read the title "DESERT HEAT". What was that doing out of her file? Staring at it, her breath caught in her chest, and her mind went to the flickering face—the studious concentration.

"Nooooooooo!"

Pulling the disk file onto her lap, she checked each disk in numbered order. Nothing was missing. Still not relieved, she removed each and examined it closely. A corner was smudged on number eight. Was that a water stain on number four? Many of her disks were very old.

It proved nothing. The man is an architect. Of course, he must spend many hours before his computer, drawing not studying. Wouldn't he use traditional means to draw his plans, on an inclined table? She really didn't know much about architects.

Why was she so upset? Of course, if he was curious, he could go to any book store or library to read her work. Why did the thought of him reading her innermost thoughts bother her? She had made them available to the public at large. Deedee had never felt the need to remain anonymous until now. She had been protected by her marriage, her friends, her hometown.

She felt a shudder of vulnerability travel up her spine.

The pounding began anew after the lunch break, reminding her of the muscled men who surrounded her. But, they faded with the sun and so did the protection of their numbers. Hadn't she just said to herself that she was not afraid of the mountain man? "Stop it, Deedee! Stop it!" she scolded herself aloud.

* * * * * *

It had taken all day to find the perfect look. Eric's suede sport coat was classic but did not make him look like an executive. The black shirt he wore open-collared beneath the tan hide was crisply starched. A slim, gold necklace caught the bathroom light beneath his manicured beard. His black slacks fit snugly on his hips; the pleats allowing room for his muscled thighs.

Eric pinned the cream carnation to his lapel and went to his jewelry box to find his dress ring. The ruby set in diamonds would add color to his earthy wardrobe.

When he lifted the lid, the old wedding band trapped his gaze. Why had he opened this box? No wonder he had left it unopened for so many years. The memories flooded back—the ruby—the color of blood. His hand shook as he lifted it away from the wedding band.

He collapsed onto his bed; his legs no longer able to support him. Eric slipped the ring onto his right hand, trembling. She had bought this for him for his birthday only two weeks before her death. He had had so little time with her: six months of wedded bliss, two years in prison with only a lost memory to sustain him, and ten years of forlorn suffering.

He looked at the corsage in the clear, plastic box on his dressing table. The orange and yellow flowers would bring out the fire in her hair.

Eric closed the jewelry box and moved to pick up the beautiful flowers. This self-torture had to end. He couldn't go on hating any longer. He couldn't play victim to the world and cower in his cabin. She had changed something deep inside of him. Deedee had drawn him out of the prison in which he had entombed himself.

His teeth flashed back to him from the mirror above the dresser. With great resolve and a little trepidation, Eric headed for the door. He felt as if his past had died with the closing of that lid. If only he could believe that. If only this wonderful woman could erase his terrible past, or, at least, relieve him of the pain of remembering.

CHAPTER FIVE

"Mr. Eric Broddery," Deedee said sarcastically as she opened the door to his knock. "Mr. Breyer told me you were his next appointment." She smiled apishly, then blushed from the pleasure of seeing him, scalding her cheeks.

Eric knew better. He had wheedled the whole story from Mr. Breyer after she had left with threats of the state's privacy policy. Eric smiled and proffered the corsage. "Would you do me the honor of accompanying me to dinner this evening—to make up for my mistreatment of you?"

Deedee felt like drooling when she paid less attention to her own remarks and more attention to what stood before her. He was god-like in his stance. His broad shoulders carried the soft suede to hang to perfection across his mounded chest. The coat was open, and the shirt was tailored to his narrow waist. She longed to rub the soft fabric and feel the solidity that lay beneath it. All of her hate, anger, tears, and fears of the day were buried in these new sensations.

"Oh, Eric, I couldn't. I haven't been able to shower for a week." She pointed to her sink—her sponge, soap, and bath towel obvious. "And I'm not dressed." She was still wearing her business suit, her feet filthy and her hosiery ripped to shreds.

"May I offer my shower?" He gleamed. "My apologies. I should have done so much earlier."

"Can I take a rain check?"

"Absolutely not. I will not accept no for an answer. This is an apology; I'm on bended knee."

"Well, you are not!" she blurted.

"Well, pretend I am. I don't want to soil my new clothes."

That sounded more like the man Deedee was beginning to know. "Oh, all right, but promise you won't humph off and leave me stranded somewhere."

Eric nearly lost his resolve. He bristled at her crude comment and stared at her agitated. He had to remember that her façade was not the real Deedee but only a layer he would peel away to expose her sensitive soul. He ignored her remark as if it had not been spoken. "May I help you carry something?"

Deedee rummaged through her drawers and closet while Poncho and Cisco, jumping on new clothing, pestered Eric for attention. Oh, no, she didn't have a new pair of hosiery. She shoved the dress back into the closet and exchanged it for her cream-satin slacks and dress-leather boots. The beaded top that matched was too seductive; the beads dragging the drape of knit across her breasts. It couldn't be helped. She didn't have anything else in pants as dressy, and Eric was dressed to perfection. She stuffed a lacy, beige, strapless bra into the knit, in case it drooped too low, and grabbed the panties that matched. Her makeup and hairbrush still in her purse, she was ready to go.

"I can handle everything just fine, thank you."

Eric almost laughed at the tennis shoes she wore with the prim suit but decided to hold his mirth at all costs. He cleared his throat instead.

* * * * * *

As Deedee showered, loving the throbbing stream massaging away dire thoughts, she hummed in contentment. This was a REAL DATE. Amy would be proud of her.

Deedee wanted to stay under the water much longer, but Eric was waiting for her. Luckily, a hair dryer lay on the counter because she had forgotten hers. She quickly dried and fluffed her curls with one hand while applying makeup with the other. Her heart raced. Was the flush on her rosy cheeks from the heat of the dryer? She applied color to the area, knowing the flush would fade no matter where it came from.

Eric's personal things lay on the counter: the cologne he wore, his hairbrush, his razor and shaving cream. Her curiosity disgracing her, she opened the medicine cabinet. There was nothing there of the personal nature she had expected. He was not prepared for the ominous, lurid acts she thought him capable of. She wondered at the discovery, but it did not ease her foreboding. Maybe, he kept them in the night stand.

"Deedee, shame on you!" she scolded her reflection.

"What did you say? Can I help you find something?"

"No! Don't come in here! I'm not dressed!" Good Lord, she was ranting like a schoolgirl. The door was locked; he hadn't tried it. He must be hovering at the door waiting for her. She quickly pulled on her clothes, not trusting the lock or Eric.

Moments later, she opened the door and was gratified by his expression.

"You look incredible, Deedee," he said, taking the corsage in his hand and holding it up to her shoulder. His other hand automatically slipped inside her top to prevent the pin from pricking her.

Eric was the one who felt the shock. The top curve of her breast gave beneath his upturned hand—soft, malleable. He took his time pinning the corsage, looking down to her face and curving bust.

Deedee looked up to him to say some smart thing like, "Need any help?" or "Get your filthy hands off of me!" or "Take a picture, it'll last longer!" but no words came from her parted lips. Eric's eyes captured her and held her entranced—shimmering, quivering jell-o.

The corsage secured, Eric turned his hand over and moved it down to the lacy barrier. He bent to take the fluttering lips with his own. Her shock kept her mouth open for his invasion. Eric's tongue tasted the sweet juices of her mouth and explored her slick teeth. Her tongue hung back, cowering. Finally, he felt its tip tickle him seductively, causing him to tense.

Eric removed his hand from its soft bed and wrapped both arms around her. Placing his hands to cup under her firm posterior, he drew her inward and upward to press against his hard arousal. She groaned into his kiss and wilted toward him, swooning in his arms, while Eric's eyes rolled beneath the lids, all control being sucked out of him by her willing flesh.

"No. Oh no, Deedee." Regretfully, he drug himself away from her, still holding her eyes locked with his while he brought his body under control. A little, devilish grin, of things to come, wavered the corners of his mouth.

"I'm starved. Are you ready to go?" he asked.

Deedee was still enthralled, and shivering, and held paralyzed by his gaze. Only when he turned away, did he partially release her from the trance.

"I...I...yes, I'm hungry," she stammered. She had never felt so unrestrained. She was silly putty to be bounced against the wall or pressed out to whatever pleasure this man desired. Now she WAS frightened—very frightened of her nonexistence as a person in his presence. She was a toy, handed over to him, to please him in any way that he wished.

Dwelling on her dilemma, Deedee didn't even know how she had gotten to the car. Nor did she know she was in the car until the old jeep door closed and she saw Eric stalk around the front. He was so dashing—a stick of dynamite ready to explode inside of her. Another shudder shook her, traveling all the way down to her...She released her breath in a long sigh of extreme vulnerability and watched him mount the seat behind the steering wheel.

Eric offered her a little reassuring smile. "There's a very nice bar and restaurant in town. It's really unique. I think you'll like it."

"I'm sure I will," she said shakily, knowing she required the length of a football field between herself and this man.

Eric wasn't fairing any better. He was having to rely on very old memories to know the right thing to say and the right thing to do. He had very nearly blown it. He could not seem to keep his hands away from her. He wanted to meld his body to hers for all eternity. Having held her and kissed her and made love to her so many times in his mind, it was difficult to separate real life from his fantasies.

Fantasies had not prepared him for the explosion of animal surge that had raced in his loins, suppressing all reason. He knew he had scared her. Why did he have to be so big and ugly and clumsy? Why couldn't he be a normal Joe like Mr. Breyer or Greg Thompson? Deedee was quivering in the corner like a captured baby rabbit. Eric took her hand to quell the quaking, knowing it would force calm back into her body.

Had she, too, felt the rightness of their being together—the inevitability of it?

* * * * * * *

Deedee was overwhelmed by the place they were entering. Huge animal heads witnessed their passing. Fires blazed behind massive hearths to take the chill from the cool mountain air. White, linen tablecloths and real silver adorned the tables. Cheerful waitresses treated them like royalty. No wonder tourists flocked back to this place. She had never seen anything quite like it. Straddled across time, it seemed to bridge and hold together the past and the present. Deedee offered Eric her delighted smile.

The bar list was brought to them for before-dinner cocktails. Deedee ordered a frilly-fruity-sounding drink and Eric ordered coffee. His expression dared her to say anything, and she just smiled.

"Eric, thank you for bringing me here. It's just unbelievably wonderful."

"Yes, it is, isn't it? I've only been here once, but it's an experience you don't soon forget. I don't want you to forget this night, Deedee—not ever."

She felt titillation at his comment. The roots of her hair tingled on her scalp, and she wondered if she had dried her hair thoroughly.

The conversation turned light when their western-sounding meal arrived. It was a scrumptious concoction of beef, mushrooms, cheddar, peppers, onions, et cetera and thrilled her palate. They talked about the construction, Cisco and Big Dog's friendly antics, the fair, cool weather, and his shopping spree. When the meal was ended, and only empty plates lay before them, Eric dropped some cash onto the tray from a roll in his pant's pocket. Maybe that was the hardness she had felt. She flushed, remembering.

Eric took her hand, startling her. She rose and followed where he led—a zombie moving to the sound of its master.

They sat at a table in the bar in front of the roaring fire. Eric thought she was cold because of her constant shivering.

"Deedee, would you like another drink to top off that great meal?"

"Oh sure, Eric," she responded, her eyes shifting away from his. The walls were full of old, framed pictures and artifacts of every description. She could avoid his devil eyes forever.

"Deedee,"—he took her hand and forced her gaze while the bartender brought their drinks, coffee and an Old Fashioned,—"I know you're recently widowed. I'm sorry if I've caused you further pain by my harsh words and actions."

Deedee glared at him head on, snatching her hand from his grasp. "How do you know I'm a widow? I've told NO ONE!"

"I have connections in Tucson."

"You've been reading my books, haven't you?" she accused.

"Would that offend you, Deedee?"

"Weeeell…n-noooo, but…" she stuttered.

"I want to read everything you've ever written, avidly. I want to know every emotion you've ever felt or dreamed of feeling. I want to know every single thought of your imagining. Deedee, you've possessed me completely."

"This is only our first date! Eric, what are you saying?"

"There isn't a first anything for us, anymore. I feel like I've been waiting on this mountain all my life for you to arrive. Celibate, frustrated, I waited for rescue. You came and effected that rescue. It couldn't have been coincidence that brought you to my house in the middle of the night— that brought you to me, Deedee. Don't you believe in fate?"

"You're MAD! Take me home right now."

"Now who's running out on whom? Do you trust me to take you home?" Eric smiled his devilish smile.

She stomped out of the bar, leaving her purse hanging, abandoned, on the chair arm. Eric settled the bill and followed her.

When he caught her, he took her arm and lifted her into the passenger seat. "Am I moving too fast, Deedee?" He heard no answer to his question and tried to break her out of her walking coma. "How long were you married?"

"Sixteen years." The answer was automatic, but she looked at him then. His face disturbed her. A mixture of sadness and betrayal seemed to torture him. Eric closed the jeep door between them and soon climbed up beside her. She couldn't bring herself to look at him again.

"My purse?!"

Eric handed her the heavy object, unspeaking.

"Thanks."

"Mmmmmmmm."

* * * * * * *

They drove the miles in silence. Deedee jumped out and flew up the stone steps before he could think of walking her to the door. Eric watched her flight. He had tried and failed so miserably to win her heart. He was a complete klutz. He went into the house and let Big Dog out to roam, envying his freedom. Eric realized that he was still in prison—a prison of his own making. The bars were tall pines surrounding him. The warden was himself. "Self" didn't satisfy him anymore. He needed Deedee.

Lying on his bed in his dressy clothing, Eric cracked the first of the three novels he had purchased at the book store in the Springs. He bought all they had that he hadn't read. Cheating her of her royalties by reading her disks was worse than stealing. He had already torn her picture from the back cover, and it stood in a frame beside his bed. Eric had turned it around when she went into his bathroom.

Thinking of her there, he went into the small room. Picking up a curly strand of hair from his shower drain, he twisted it around his finger. He smelled her fragrance on the still-damp towel. Loving was killing, and he had it bad.

"Deeeeeedeeeee!!"

* * * * * * *

The eerie sound stopped her in her tracks when she was bringing Cisco around the cabin for his nightly need. "Oh, Eric. What am I doing to you? What are you doing to me?"

CHAPTER SIX

The day was too busy for the mountain man to enter Deedee's mind. The plumber was there, and he was hooking up the toilet to the new septic system. She would have a shower, and a bathroom sink, and a toilet that flushed. The stars would still be her ceiling. The roofless/windowless room was far from completion as far as the walls and floors went, but the facilities would soon be serviceable. Oh, but it would be heaven to have her own bathroom. The door was on and had a lock. Someone would have to climb a tree to spy on her. Because she didn't put that past anyone, she would use caution when entering the little room.

The electrician arrived and connected her mirror lights and shower light. Thrilled, Deedee danced in the tiny room, getting in everyone's way. All that remained was the beamed ceiling, the staining, the plush carpet for her bedroom, and the fireplace. And, the windows and sliding door. That was an awful lot left to do. Deedee's happy dance stopped and her heart sank. Her goal had seemed so close.

The carpenters were cutting a hole in the wall between this unfinished room and her living room. She tried to shout over the sound of their saws but couldn't get their attention. She ran to find Greg. He was supervising the unloading of the roof trusses and seemed more than annoyed by her agonized interruption.

"Greg, your men are cutting a hole in my wall. I won't be able to lock up tonight."

"The man is coming to install the firebox this afternoon. This was the only day we could schedule him. He'll do the masonry, too. You should have a completed fireplace by tomorrow noon."

"But what about tonight? How will I lock my house?"

"We'll scoot something in front of it like we always do. Don't worry about it, Deedee."

Greg put his arm around her shoulder as if to comfort her. She shrugged him off.

"When will that damn latch be here, Greg? It's been over a week."

"Hell, Deedee, that latch is a two-way anyway. How would that help?"

"It might keep animals out. These ARE the woods, you know!" She stomped off.

Needing her work to calm her, she began writing at her computer. The noisy construction faded to the background of her mind. She typed, and typed, and typed. Cisco jumped into her lap and cried pathetically. "Not now, Cisco." He persisted. She turned to scold him and saw the darkness of the room. Only the insect sounds of the forest met her ears.

She had done it again. Lost in the story of her mind, she had let real life pass by unnoticed.

Cisco and Poncho must be starved—she was. She switched on the kitchen light and found the canned food.

Then, she saw the black hole gaping, the bureau sitting in the corner. Having to move the heavy piece herself would be a horrible task, but she would have to try rather than ask the mountain man.

Deedee hurried to put the animals' food on the floor. The only reason Poncho hadn't escaped through the fireplace hole was that he didn't know it was there. He was still sound asleep curled up atop the warmth of her computer screen. Deedee fetched the toasty bundle and laid him in one of her desk drawers.

There had been a time, when he was smaller, he could have slipped through the back cracks of a drawer. But no longer. He was now too fat and lazy, and had lost a lot of the dexterity he had had in his youth. He had been her friend and companion long before Cisco came on the scene. The name "Poncho" was derived from the garment she wore when she brought the tiny baby home, wrapped up in its warmth. When the black Poodle was given to her as a Christmas gift from Daniel, "Cisco" seemed the only name possible for the instant friends.

She had to scoot one corner of the dresser at a time to move the heavy piece of furniture across the lumpy wood floor. She took drawers out, and it didn't help. She took hanging clothes out, and it didn't help. Taking an eternity, she finally maneuvered the piece in place in front of the gaping fireplace hole.

Now, she had a further problem. The bedroom door had no latch and no bureau. Having to go to the bathroom, anyway, after the long hours of writing, she opened the two doors simultaneously. She noticed they met in a triangle of light, closing out the dark, open bedroom. If she could only connect them somehow.

Finishing in the glorious luxury of a real bathroom, Deedee went for Cisco's leash and looped it around the doorknob. She ran it to the center hinge on the kitchen door, and—voilà—they were connected. They bounced a bit from the length of the leash, but the tie off should work. Her only threat would now be bats flying in over the top of the door.

She went to the wall that was her kitchen to find food; her stomach growling like a grizzly bear's. There, she was doing it again. Everything she said seemed to remind her of Eric.

Almost forgetting Poncho, she let him out of the drawer and took another bite from her sandwich.

Turning on the radio for a little noise, she heard the broadcaster giving the news. "My God, it's past ten o'clock." The day had passed so fast. Snapping off the radio, she pulled one of her old books off the shelf and started to read. She found herself wanting to make corrections on the published copy. Frustrated, she shoved it back in its slot. Who was she trying to kid? All she could think about was the man and his pain, the man and his everything.

Walking to the edge of her balcony, she looked down on him. His bedroom windows faced her. The house was dark. Not even the glow of a computer screen broke the carpet of black.

Disappointment ate away at her insides. She wanted to assure herself that he was all right. The wrenching cry of her name the previous night had pulled something within her. She had tried to block him from her torpid brain with outside stimulation throughout the day. But it hadn't worked. The man who prowled through the mountains in her new book and hungered for her new heroine was him.

Deedee had spent this day with him as surely as if he had been right beside her.

If he hadn't stopped that passionate kiss, she would have let him possess her completely. He had said that Deedee possessed him, but it hadn't felt that way, quite the opposite. She had been drunk in the wine of his kiss and would have passed out in his arms—willing—wanting.

What had caused her to become a sex toy, unable to control a simple kiss? What had caused her distress? Was it because Daniel wasn't here to relieve her of her self-induced, sexual arousal? Had she used him only for that purpose during their long marriage?

That was ridiculous. How could she even think such a thing? And, yet, didn't everyone in a marriage use their partner in one way or another? Hadn't Daniel demanded that she be the perfect hostess: flashing a fresh drink to every empty, bowing, and scraping, and brilliantly coming up with clever idioms.

This self-examination was destroying her morals and morale. If Deedee truly stayed with Daniel only for her own gratification, she would have to stop writing romances and resort to murder mysteries. But if writing a romance drove her to any man's bed who kissed her, what would murder mysteries do?

Deedee prepared for bed in a short, light, cotton gown. That was all she had brought. It was supposed to be summer, after all. Her grandmother's quilt kept her warm and cozy on the double bed, but she hoped to put it on the wall or over the corner of the couch to preserve it. Right now, she needed its warmth. The bright design was so original, and it was irreplaceable. When the fireplace was finished, she could move it.

She had just settled into a comfortable position when she noticed that Cisco wasn't curled up beside her for his tummy rub. Switching on the bedside light, she looked around her. Cisco was standing, expectantly, at the front door. Having just eaten, he needed to relieve himself. Groaning her complaint at leaving the warm cover, Deedee got out of bed.

Cisco's leash was still on the door barrier that she had created. She would just have to do everything all over again. If she took him out without the leash, he would bolt for the woods, and Deedee didn't intend to lose any sleep crashing through the woods to retrieve him.

She untied the inventive lock and took Cisco outside. It was so dark. She would have to see about installing outdoor lighting. Skirting the cabin, she walked to the hill in the back to take advantage of the light reflecting off her patio and to glance one more time down the hill to the darkened cabin beneath her.

Deedee heard a commotion. Was Eric crashing around in the dark down there, afraid that she was watching?

After Cisco peed on every weed and squatted, Deedee led him back to the cabin door. The cold air had penetrate her bones. She would have to buy a thick robe, especially when winter crept near.

She opened the door to, "AAAAAAAAAAAA!!!" she screamed.

Cisco lunged on the end of his leash, and Deedee dragged him, unceremoniously, down beside her, slamming the door. She ran to the incline and, grabbing Cisco up in her arms, scooted painfully down the hill.

A huge bear had been sitting on her couch, right by the door. Its lower jaw had yawed back and forth with the thrashing of its massive head. Its white stiletto teeth were bared with its mouth agape in growling rage. A second bear had taken possession of her bed and pulled at her grandmother's quilt, also bawling at her intrusion.

If Cisco hadn't been on his leash, he would probably now be dead. The fearless little animal would have attacked the bears for invading his territory. However, if it weren't for Cisco's leash, the bears couldn't have gotten in there in the first place. She had removed it from the flopping, unlatched door.

"Poncho!!" she exhaled as her hands scrapped cinders. "Poncho's still in there!" Deedee couldn't go back for him. "Please let Poncho be safe, curled up under the desk or dresser. Please, please."

* * * * * * *

His door was unlocked—his back door—the one closest to her shaking fingers. She cried his name, "Eric! E-e-eeric!"

"Here!"

Deedee ran into his bedroom, into the pool of light he had provided for her. Leftover sleep sagged his face. She saw her own face, in a frame, staring back at her from his night stand. Too upset for anything to register on her shaky mind, she set Cisco down and fled to him.

"Bears!!! Eric, giant bears!!"

She was shaking visibly when he wrapped his arms around her frightened, fragile body. Like a leaf in the wind, every extremity trembled.

Eric stood, holding her tight against him, each curve and valley of her easily felt through her thin apparel and his thin boxers. It took every vow he had ever made in his life to prevent him from taking her now. "Oh, God!" he said and pushed her away to arms length, holding her shoulders.

Trying to recover his elusive composure, he tried to calm her. "Deedee, those bears lived in your cabin last winter. As far as they're concerned, you're the trespasser."

"Do you have a gun? Can you get them OUTTA MY HOUSE?!" Her voice rose two octaves in rage and terror.

"How many were there?"

"Two!!"

"Okay, calm down. Sit here," he said, sinking down onto the bed and indicating the spot beside him.

She sat down and, realizing where she was, bolted back up again.

Eric held her arm and drew her back down. Ignoring her defensive behavior he continued to explain. "Those are the cubs."

"Cubs?!!!! They were HUGE!!!"

"Was one more huge than the other?"

"Noooooo," she said meekly.

"Then the mother's not there. If the mother had been there, you probably wouldn't have escaped with your life, Deedee. She would have viciously defended her cubs." He held her against the shiver his words caused. "My guess is that the mother has abandoned them. They should be old enough to live on their own. If she did, they're just as frightened as you are. They came to THEIR home, THEIR den, to look for her."

"Can you kill them—shoot them?"

"Do you really want that? Deedee, I've never killed a living creature in my life."

Deedee watched his mouth freeze into a hard line. He was staring at his open palms resting against his furry legs. Why did everything she say seem to upset him? He must hate killing. "No, I don't want them dead, just gone. What can I dooooo?" she mewed.

He turned and embraced her tightly in his arms, their bare legs touching, sitting side by side on the edge of the bed and the edge of reality. Another tremor shook her, not from her dilemma but from his close proximity. She could smell pine on him, mixed with the sweet scent of his cologne. For a trembling moment, she wanted that hard line of a mouth to take her, devour her in its anger and animal hunger.

"Stay here tonight, Deedee. You can sleep on the couch in the living room. You have before."

"Poncho's in there, alone, afraid. Oh, Eric, I'm so terrified they'll find him and eat him."

"Deedee, they're brown bears, not grizzlies for God's sake. They eat berries and roots and honey. Think about Winnie the Pooh."

Deedee couldn't help it. She broke into peals of nervous laughter at his silliness. "'Winnie the Pooh,'" Another laugh shook her, this one more relaxed, replacing the shaking of her fear. "Thanks, Eric, you've made me feel better."

He gave her another assuring squeeze and released her, dropping his arm back to his lap, abandoned of its soft fulfillment. "They should leave as soon as the sun comes up. They'll probably raid your cabinets and sleep off the feast. If we tried to dislodge them, they would just tear your place apart in the process."

Cisco jumped up on the bed beside Deedee, demanding her attention. No one seemed to notice his terror and trembling body.

"Oh, Cisco, you poor thing," Deedee said, lifting him to her lap to soothe him. She kissed him profusely and received his licking response, sending waves of jealousy pulsing through Eric's body.

Eric rose and went to his closet, taking down a large, fluffy blanket. Its pink flowers looked out of place in his hairy arms and rustic house. Deedee accepted it from him and, again, saw her face in the frame when he reached across his bed for the spare pillow.

Somehow IT didn't look out of place, and she said nothing about its being there. "Thanks," she said, getting up. "Good night, Eric. Thank you for making me feel more at ease."

Eric snapped off the light when he heard her settle on the couch. He threw his arm across his forehead, and stared blindly at the dark beams of the ceiling. He smiled.

* * * * * * *

Deedee awoke to the smell of coffee and the sound of crackling bacon. Cisco was sitting up beside her, sniffing the wonderful aroma.

A scratch at the door brought Eric striding across the room—bare-chested, spatula in hand—to let Big Dog in.

Deedee sat up in defense as the bounding monster's wagging body approached her and Cisco. Realizing the sparsity of her attire, she pulled the floral blanket up to surround her.

Eric walked back to the kitchen without a word. The louvered screen had been drawn back so he could watch her while he cooked. She had looked like an angel with her lashes resting against her freckled cheeks, and lacy tendrils of hair shading her eyes from the sun streaks coming in the window.

"Why didn't you tell me I was so scantily dressed?" she asked, her voice roguishly rough from sleep.

"It never entered my mind, Deedee. Good morning."

"WHAT never entered your mind, my scanty apparel or telling me?"

"Both. I mean neither. Are you hungry? Coffee?"

Nice change of subject, Eric Broddery, she thought. "Eric, do you have something I can put on?" She had expected him to offer. He hadn't. She didn't intend to wear a blanket to breakfast.

He went to his bedroom and brought her the black shirt. She slipped into the bathroom and came out a few minutes later wearing the shirt over her gown. It hung to mid thigh and covered her decently. The male musk smell of him was still intertwined with the fabric and was driving her crazy. He probably hadn't washed it, having worn it only once. A man without a woman would wear a garment until it stood by itself in the corner, or so she believed. Thank heaven, the smell of coffee and bacon finally overpowered the masculine scent.

A small table was set in the kitchen; the coffee poured in china cups. Deedee sat down, and Eric carried two plates to the table, heaped with scrambled eggs, hash browns, bacon, and toast.

"Oh, that smells so good. Thank you, Eric. I haven't had someone cook me breakfast since I was a girl." Her comment made it clear that it was something her husband would never have thought of doing.

"I'm glad to have remedied that." He smiled and headed for the door. Big Dog was scratching to get outside to play with Cisco.

Eric was half way across the room before Deedee understood what he was doing. "NO! Eric, the bears!" She tried to recover some of her composure. "Please don't let them out until we know the bears are gone," she pleaded.

"Sorry, Deedee. Big Dog can hold his own against bears. I didn't think."

"Oh, Poncho," she said, crushing her napkin into her fist. She looked at the wonderful breakfast. Sick to her stomach with worry at the thought of Poncho alone and frightened, she got up from the table. "I'm the one who's sorry, Eric. You've gone to all this trouble. I have to go. I have to find Poncho. Can Cisco stay here with you until it's safe?"

"You aren't going up there alone, Deedee. Wait here."

Once again she didn't dream of ignoring his demand. A few minutes later, he came from his bedroom carrying a ball bat.

"I'm so stupid, fixing that breakfast while you were so worried about your weasel."

"It's a ferret, Eric. You're not alone, though. Everyone thinks it rather strange that I could love a weasel."

Eric looked at her oddly, not sure how to unravel her words. He thought he knew everything about her, but right now, he was puzzled. Why would she correct him and then use the same wrong euphemism? Was there more meaning to her statement? Was he the weasel? Was her husband the weasel? It made no sense. She was probably just talking about her ferret, and he was trying to make a declaration of love out of it.

His large hand engulfed hers as he pulled her up the hill. She was still shaking, but he didn't know the real reason for her distress.

Deedee hung back when he opened the door to her cabin, fearful of what she might see.

"They're gone, Deedee."

She burst in ahead of him, calling for Poncho and looking under boxes on the kitchen floor and blankets surrounding the bed. Her hand went under every piece of furniture, searching for his furry warmth.

Eric just stood watching, filling his eyes with her bouncing rump and bare legs. She seemed oblivious of his scrutiny in her frantic, luscious activity.

"Eric, don't just stand there. Help me look."

They combed the place together. There was no sign of Poncho. Deedee stood in the center of destruction and, dropping her arms in complete defeat, wailed like a broken baby doll.

Eric walked over to her. A tear ran down his cheek from watching her pain. Her pain became his. He wrapped her up and held her as close as he could without crushing her. He crooned, "It'll be all right, Deedee. He probably ran away. The house was open. That's okay, Baby."

Greg arrived on the hill with his work crew. Looking through the door at the wreckage, he saw Deedee crying. "What's going on here? Deedee, are you all right?!"

Eric's head turned and he scowled at Greg, then snarled like an animal. Greg backed away with both hands up and went back to join his workers.

Eric thought of the construction. "Deedee, we didn't check the new rooms."

They both ran through the unlatched door to meet the astonished stares of the carpenters. Eric walked around the littered room, looking behind boards, and sawdust piles, and in tool boxes.

"He's here!" Deedee yelled from the bathroom.

Eric ran to find Deedee sitting on the floor, grinning and rocking her ferret. The ferret hung limply from her hand in sleepy wonder.

"Oh, Eric, he's probably been here all night. I had the doors connected. He crawled under the cabinet and got up through the pipe hole." Deedee giggled in glee to have her animal safe in her arms."

"Thank God," Eric said unsmiling, jealousy once again burning for the love she lavished on this small creature. "Do you want to finish that breakfast? You have to retrieve Cisco anyway."

"Yes, oh yes. Let me get dressed first."

"Why, Deedee? We've already shocked the hell out of every man on this mountain. What difference could it make?"

Deedee's pleased smile faded, and her mind clicked in gear. What must this look like to the men. Good Lord! The whole place was a wreck. Here she sat wearing his shirt, and him bare-chested very early in the morning. Embarrassment flushed her. She stood up and squared her shoulders, shouting for all to hear.

"Ha! They'll just think I practice what I preach!"

She walked proudly out the door, carrying Poncho, with Eric following in shock. The lady's got balls, he thought, grinning, a shred of worry and protectiveness tickling the back of his mind. He turned and glared at the gawking men with fire in his eyes, daring any one of them to say or do what they were thinking.

* * * * * *

Eric refried the potatoes and eggs, left the bacon cold, put the toast down for the animals, and replaced the cold coffee with hot. Deedee watched with appreciation for his proficiency. She would have had a hard time scraping together an edible meal from the cold breakfast.

They dug into the food together. Stress, worry, and exercise had stirred up their insatiable hunger. They ate until every itty-bitty-bit of food was demolished, and then relaxed against the backs of their chairs in contentment.

Deedee laughed at Poncho. His back was arched high, and he was lunging forward and jumping backward in front of Big Dog, who just ignored him.

"Oh, Eric, look. He would have done the same thing to the bears. Thank God for his laziness."

"I'm glad everything turned out satisfactorily for you, Deedee. I'll see that you get framed in today. The roof will have to wait. Once the windows and sliding door are in, you should be safe from bears." The thought of her danger from something other than bears worried him. He would do his best to make her safe from all dangers.

"It's all Greg's fault. I've told him several times that I couldn't lock that door. He said he would take care of it, and he left without even blocking the fireplace last night. I had to move that chest myself." She remembered being lost inside her computer. "I guess I'm just as much to blame. I was writing and didn't even notice when they left."

"It's senseless to place blame. We just have to make sure it doesn't happen again. I wouldn't mind if you would like to stay here until they've finished up there. It'll only be another week." Oh, and what a wonderful week that would be. Eric cherished the thought of sharing his home with her.

"No, I've caused you enough trouble."

"Trouble? Deedee, everything you do or say troubles me. This distraction was a relief."

Confused by what he said—Why did he have to be so enigmatic?—Deedee drank the last of her coffee. When she finished, she carried both of their plates to the sink. "Let me do the dishes since you did the cooking."

"No, leave them. I'll help you clean up the mess the bears left. These can wait."

Deedee let Cisco run free with Big Dog and carried Poncho up the steps. Eric's hand was bracing her firmly on her back. The contact was affecting her after all that had happened: the terror of the night, the loss she felt for Poncho, the comfort he had given to her insane plight.

She thought about him holding her, nearly nude in the skimpy gown. His control was incredible. They were on his bed, half dressed. She had been blubbering all over him. How had he managed to resist? Maybe, he didn't want her any longer after the stupid stunt she had pulled at the bar.

A shiver ran down her back. Eric felt it against his hand. "You're cold. I'm sorry, Deedee, I could have, at least, let you put on your shoes."

Deedee looked down at her bare feet and laughed brokenly. "I didn't even know I was barefoot."

Her laugh sounded more like hysteria than laughter. "Are you all right?" he asked.

"No! I'm anything but all right! Why does everyone keep asking me that?"

"Deedee, I have to go talk to Greg. They're starting the roof. I'll be right back."

"Huh? Sure," she said, her voice edgy.

"Deedee, I won't leave you if you need me."

"Need you? Need you? I don't need you, Eric. I'm going to be a hermit just like you." She stomped across the small porch and slammed the door hard behind her.

All Eric could do was stare at the wood. He didn't know quite what had happened. Was that so unusual? Every minute he spent with this woman just added one more piece to the puzzle. He shrugged and walked toward Greg. Maybe someday all of the pieces would be put together, and he could look at the lovely, feminine, work-of-art their combination created.

* * * * * * *

Deedee moaned at the mess that faced her and what she had done. Why had she done that? Why had she lashed out at him? It was because she thought he didn't want her. She had thought she was running from one bear to another last night. She just happened to know the grizzly bear's name, so he was safer. Of course, he was safer; he didn't want her.

Flinging the covers back on the bed, she tried to straighten them. No use, they were horribly stained. She ripped them off and went to the dresser to get more sheets. She saw the fireplace guy peering at her through the metal box, trowel and mortar in hand. Glaring back at him, she slammed the drawer shut.

Eric came through the flopping door of the addition, carrying several boards and some hardware and drill. He didn't look at her, nor speak, but busied himself, hammering and drilling. By the time Deedee had made the bed, he was finished with his busy industry."Come here, Deedee," he demanded her cold expression.

She came—any other reaction unthinkable. Looking at the result of his work, her mouth fell open. "Thank you," she mumbled.

The latch was truly wonderful. The wood bars, on both sides of the door, lifted on the pivot bolt and rested in the cradle on the door casing. There was even a hole to push a peg in to keep the latch from lifting—an effective lock. Deedee strutted up to Greg.

"Cancel the order for the door latch. I have no need for it."

Greg just leered at her. There was no other word to describe that look.

She went back into her living room and latched the door. Eric had gone. Good God! She was still in her night gown, barefoot, and wearing Eric's shirt! No wonder Greg had leered. She gathered some clothing and went to the bathroom to change, locking the door behind her. Dressing in the shower stall, she still watched for peepers through the frosted door. After her stupid statement this morning, she would be lucky not to be raped before the day was done.

Dressed in baggy shorts and a summer sweater, tennies on her feet, she went to the horrid kitchen and started putting up boxes and cans that had fallen to the floor. Cisco knocked, and she let him in. Thinking then of Poncho, she looked for him. The firebox gaped at her; the door had been open for Eric's repairs. Had she gone through all of this to lose Poncho by her own irresponsible behavior? He was not to be found.

Deedee started asking the men. The man laying masonry had not seen Poncho escape through the firebox. Finally, one of the men, installing a window, said he had seen the ferret headed toward the woods. He hadn't known it was a pet. He pointed toward the trees where the ferret had entered.

Heartsick, Deedee went to get Cisco and put him on his leash. "Find Poncho," she ordered. Did she think he was a bloodhound?

Relieved when Cisco entered the woods where the man had pointed, she followed the straining leash. She was falling apart with anguish. She had to pull herself together. Putting her animals at risk by her infantile behavior was intolerable.

Her search was thorough. No bush nor tree went unscanned for a sleeping ferret. "Poncho," she called. "Come here, Poncho. Where are you, you ornery critter?"

Cisco led her into deep woods. Brambles and twigs were catching her sweater and scratching her legs. She continued to call Poncho. Praying that she and Cisco were not lost, praying that Cisco, indeed, was following Poncho's trail, she didn't see the old board under the thick brush—the board that had taken Cisco's weight so easily.

CHAPTER SEVEN

Eric went to his drafting table to put a few final touches on his latest design. This work would give him time to try to understand Deedee. The morning had been perfect for him, even though it hadn't been for her. Giving her comfort and helping her meant a great deal to him. Surely, soon, she would see how much he loved her.

Restless, he went outside and looked up at her patio. There were a few carpenters adjusting the sliding door that had just been hung. Eric waved when they glanced down at him. He saw some wild flowers growing near her braces and went to pick them. How could she resist him if he came bearing flowers. She had had time to calm down from whatever upset her that morning. He had to risk it. He wanted to see her desperately, to hear her voice, to hold her hand. These simple things were enough for him if she was feeling pressured. He would slow down and give her time.

"Where's Deedee?" Eric asked cordially, a bouquet of wild flowers clutched, ridiculously, in his fist.

"I don't know," Greg answered.

"Her car's here. Where is she?" Eric persisted.

"Any of you guys see Deedee?" Greg shouted.

"She went to look for that ferret." One of the carpenters pointed to the woods where she had entered.

Eric asked the man, "When did she leave?"

"Shortly after you did."

"Greg, that was this morning. We have to try to find her." Eric's fears for the small woman in the mighty forest forced the blood pumping to the veins in his forehead. He threw down the flowers.

"Mr. Broddery, I can't leave the site. My boss would have my ass on a platter."

Eric grabbed the man by his collar, raising him off the ground. "We've got to FIND HER!" he reiterated.

Greg's face, ashen, shrunk back away from the fiery breath, and he blurted, "She's gone out there before. She ain't lost."

Eric put the man down and turned his back. He needed to find Big Dog and whistled for him while he went to get a rope. He thought of Deedee's love for the ferret, Deedee searching the woods, upset, crying—Deedee lost, alone, afraid of bears—shivering from cold and fright.

Big Dog was standing on the porch wagging when Eric came from his cabin with the rope. Scolding the animal because he backed away from the hated item, Eric finally managed to slip it securely around his neck.

"Big Dog, find Cisco. Find Deedee." Eric saw the men breaking for dinner as he topped the hill to follow Big Dog into the woods. "Damn them to Hell," he cursed.

Unaccustomed to the rope lead, Big Dog plunged into the woods, overpowering even Eric's strong muscles in his anxiety to find his friend. Eric stumbled behind, trying to keep up with the rampaging beast. The thick growth slowed them both. With the sounds of construction restarting behind him, Eric knew he had already been searching for an hour. The realization depressed him, but he would not give up until Deedee was safe in his sight once again.

Fighting the strangling forest, Eric went rigid. He saw Big Dog raise his head and cock his ears, listening. The excited animal thrust forward, yanking the rope from Eric's fist.

Hurrying to follow, Eric also heard it—Cisco's yapping, whining, yapping, barking. Striving to keep up with Big Dog, in his panic, Eric let the forest rip at his legs and clothing, heedless of injury.

"DEEEEEEEDEEEEEE!!!" he screamed when he saw the little dog alone, dancing and barking at their approach.

Big Dog stared at the ground and howled.

"Eric?"

Eric heard a faint voice, so far away, so weak and frightened. He stared down the hole at her dirty face, her bright blue eyes, like tiny topaz gems, staring up at him.

"My God, Deedee!" he groaned, looking hurriedly around him for something to reach her with. Would the rope on Big Dog reach?

When he called Big Dog to him, Big Dog jumped up on him, begging him to get her out. Eric went off balance from the giant animal. His foot slipped into the hole. He grabbed frantically at the loose boards and loose weeds, dragging them all into the hole with him.

"Look ooooouut!" he hollered as he fell, scraping his length on the rough slide downward.

"Damn it, damn it, damn it, damn it," he blasted her when she came to help him from the ground. "I'm so DAMN useless!"

Deedee chuckled at their predicament, happy that she was no longer alone in the hole. He looked so silly: weeds in both hands and wood chips caught in his beard. "Jim Dandy to the rescue." She held her sides in hearty laughter.

He didn't find anything funny and glared at her with his black eyes, daring her to continue her hilarity.

Deedee found that even more hilarious and kept on. Sputtering, Eric spit a tiny laugh, and, finally, both of them were rocking in great guffaws.

"What do you think of your night-in-shining-armor, in as much distress as the damsel?" he asked, still smirking.

The smile dropped out of existence on Deedee's face, turned off like a clap switch. "Did Mr. Breyer tell you what I said?" She stared at him and lambasted ahead when he didn't answer the question. "Oh, of course he did! You're his client, and he would want to please you. Why would he care about some crazy lady who came to his office?"

"Deedee, I hardly think that matters now. We have to think of a way to get out of here."

"Oh, it matters. I want the truth, Eric Broddery. Have you been sneaking my disks? Have you been reading my computer?" Deedee thought of the things she had written about the mountain man—the same man in every way as the one who stood before her. Her cheeks flamed in embarrassment and her freckles went livid red with the thought of him reading it.

"Yes, Penelope."

"Damn you…you…you bastard!" She tore into him, her little fists beating uselessly against his strong chest. "Ooooooooooo!" she said, too mad for words. Clinching her fists, she turned her back on him. Her current hatred and anger sent vibrations through her frame. Big Dog and Cisco were both barking and growling and lunging at the hole, distraught at their battling masters.

"Big Dog, go for help! Now!"

Deedee looked up after Eric's harsh command. Big Dog was gone, but Cisco was still there. He was refusing to leave Penelope…ah…Deedee.

"Have you calmed yourself?" Eric asked.

"Yes." Her back still faced him. She was hiding the mud on her face where her frustrated tears had mixed with dirt.

Eric looked morbidly at her back. It was ironic that once again he had failed completely to help the woman he loved. He had been totally helpless to help Christine. That, more than anything else, was what had caused him so much pain. No one could believe that he had been overwhelmed. Even strength cannot stop a bullet. Would that it could. Had he known what they would do, he would have taken the bullet rather than live through that agony—her agony.

The memories that haunted his mind had been slower in coming since Deedee came to this mountain. If he just weren't trapped in this mine. It was close, confining—too much like a closet. Oh, God, the closet. Make the memories leave him. God help him. He couldn't think about the closet—not now—not here.

* * * * * * *

When Big Dog got back to the construction, no one was there. The sun had just set behind the mountain. He barked and banged on the door, but no one answered.

He headed down the road. He knew where there were people to help. Just down the road and across the bridge, he would find people.

Everyone in Green Mountain Falls would remember the night the giant dog invaded their peaceful community. He hit every place a light was shining, dragging his rope, barking, running back and forth, trying to get someone to follow.

What was wrong with these people? Hadn't they seen Lassie? Big Dog slipped through the door at the antiquated restaurant and bar, knocking over tables, sending silver and china flying, slapping laps with his big paw.

"Hey, isn't that the hermit's dog?"

"Yeah, I've seen him in that black jeep."

"He never runs loose. Not here, anyway."

"Look. He wants us to follow him."

"Reckon something's happened to the hermit?"

"One way to find out!"

Big Dog watched as many men followed his excited pleas and got into their cars. They waited for him to lead them from the parking lot—waited for Big Dog to point the way.

Running back up the highway, stopping traffic on all sides, Big Dog took them to his beloved master. Across the bridge, over the falls, and down the long blacktop—tumbling, occasionally from the speed of his furious flight—Big Dog ran with many cars in his wake. Their headlights kept him in their beams, spotlighting his thundering path.

He came to the turnaround, and still they followed, getting out of their cars with flashlights, shouting, "Hermit! Hermit!" Big Dog led them up the mountain, through the choking brush, to where Cisco guarded sentry. Panting at his tremendous exertion and amazing venture, Big Dog laid on the ground and received Cisco's welcoming licks.

* * * * * * *

But, before Big Dog reached them, before the shouts of searching men, darkness fell in the pit. This mine shaft had long since been filled in and covered over. The intersecting tunnels were no longer there. Eric and Deedee stood in an area eight by eight with sheer walls on all sides. At one time, a lift probably transported men in and out of the mine through this shaft. Eric never knew it existed, though he knew that many such mines interlaced the subterranean areas of the Colorado mountains, long stripped of their precious metals.

They were both sitting with their backs to the cold, earth wall. Having tried to climb the steep pit and even piggyback out, they had given up in exhaustion.

Deedee heard a low moan come from Eric. It was a tragic sound. The moans continued, and she moved over to him and wrapped her arms around his wracking body. A tear hit her arm—another.

"What's wrong, Eric?" she asked cautiously. It seemed a stupid question under the circumstances. "Eric, snap out of it!"

Shudders continued to wrack him. All she could do was hold onto him and try to give him comfort. This frightened her more than anything that had happened to her thus far. To see this strong man so helpless and in agony was more than she could bear.

"Are you claustrophobic?" Deedee was very much aware of the condition since she had done extensive research on it for a novel.

"Yes," he groaned.

"Talk to me, Eric. Fight with me. Kiss me. Do something—anything—to get your mind off of it."

Nothing seemed to help him. He would be in convulsions, shock, if she let this continue. Deedee pressed her open mouth against his trembling lips—so cold. She slipped her hand beneath his shirt and kneaded his back. Moving to position herself on his lap, she felt his quivering muscles begin to relax.

Her tongue explored his mouth, seeking his, and he gave it to her. His shaking fingers felt like butterfly wings as they slid up her sweater and surrounded her breast, searching for access through the thin lace barrier of her bra.

He moaned a different type of moan, and Deedee felt his hard arousal press her toward him.

"Oh, God, Eric."

His name uttered in a whisper blew her warm breath into his open mouth. Their tongues touched and circled each other's in the open space between them, and Deedee melted back toward him, whimpering when his fingers found her puckered flesh. His other hand released the fabric binding her and moved to engulf her other breast.

Eric pressed her backward and lifted her with his knees. His tongue swabbed her lusciously—the rough, wet, swirling tongue—while his soft beard tickled her tender flesh.

Deedee was clutching his head, pulling it firmly against her, demanding his teasing bite. Her breath was coming in harsh pants. She felt the loss of his hardness in her higher position. Wanting to feel him again, she sought him.

Eric's groan was very animalistic as she grasped him. He had lost all control; his need coursing through every vein in his body. He lowered her and began to tear at her shorts, desperate to have her, struggling to hold back his surging semen.

Crashing, barking, Big Dog, Cisco, lights flashing above the hole, Eric stood and pulled her with him, their bodies both still throbbing with their heat.

"Deedee," Eric growled, "Holy Christ, Deedee, marry me."

There wasn't time for an answer as the pit filled with light.

* * * * * * *

"You should have seen that dog of yours. He must have hit every bar in town," one man said.

"Yeah, he led a whole parade of cars out here, running hell-bent-for-leather," another man said.

"Never seen anything like it this side of Hollywood," the barber said. "Jim and Tom went to get ropes. Are either of you hurt?"

"NO!!!" Eric snapped hatefully.

Deedee poked him with her elbow. "We're both a little shaken,"—not a lie. "Is Big Dog with you, and the Poodle?"

"Yeah, they're both here. That big dog is lying with his tongue hanging out. He must have run ten miles to town and back. It's just not to be believed!"

Eric's and Deedee's rescuers continued to give them details of Big Dog's heroic trip to town until the ropes arrived.

A sling was tied to one end, and the rope was lowered into the pit. Eric helped to fasten Deedee snugly into the sling and held her away from the wall as long as he could reach her.

When Eric joined her in the freedom of the night, he looked around for her. Finding Deedee kneeling on the ground beside Big Dog, he knelt beside her. A strangled sound wrenched from Eric's throat.

Big Dog's breathing was shallow and rapid. His eyes didn't meet his master's when Eric bent over his head. Big Dog's tail lifted, listlessly, and fell in weak wags when he heard his master's voice, safe and near him.

Cisco licked Big Dog's ears and nudged him with his nose, trying to bring animation back into the giant limbs.

Eric picked up the huge animal, an incredible task as Big Dog had to weigh very close to two hundred pounds. The animal had tried to stand, but his legs had not held him. His tongue was hanging out and dripping; his fur wet with sweat. Refusing help on all sides, Eric carried his beloved pet the whole distance back to his cabin.

They walked in silence. All of them were aware of Eric's anguish. The excitement of the rescue was diminished by the pain of this courageous animal and his mourning master.

After Deedee had helped Eric and Big Dog enter their cabin, she went back to the turnaround. The men evaporated into their separate cars after Deedee had whispered her thanks to them. She followed Eric into his living room where he had put Big Dog down on the couch.

"Eric, should you call a veterinarian?"

"They can't do anything, Deedee. It's old age that afflicts him. If I hadn't sent him for help, this wouldn't have happened."

Eric bent and rubbed the dog's head, unable to do anything but stare into the weary eyes.

"I'm so sorry," Deedee whispered. "If I hadn't gone to the woods…"

"Damn it, Deedee! No one's to blame! Not you, not me! He's old. He's tired of living." Eric's voice trailed off with the weight of what he was saying. "He'll need sleep—rest. You go on home."

"Good night, Eric."

Deedee strode solemnly across the expanse of ground in front of her cabin. A ray of moonlight cast shadows from a pile of withered wildflowers. She lifted them. Had Eric brought these to her? She moved to her door.

Poncho was lying curled on the upper step, and Cisco pushed him with his nose as if mad for all the trouble the creature had caused. Picking Poncho up, Deedee went into the cabin.

It was warm. The remainder of a log glowed orange in the fireplace. *The fireplace man must have had to check the draft,* she thought absently.

The room was still a shambled mess, thanks to the bears. One thing after another seemed to plague her. Nothing had gone right since she came here. Was she out of her element in these mountains? Eric probably wished she hadn't come. She had tormented the man with her constant problems and, now, with unsatisfied sexual desires. Deedee noticed the ball bat still standing by the door.

Going into the empty bedroom, she gathered some broken boards. Finally, the windows were all up, and the sliding door blocked bears and bobcats. She brought the wood fragments and put them on the glowing coals. They caught and leaped into live flame.

The fireplace was beautiful; the natural stone made it look massive. How long had she yearned for this fire? Now that she had it, it had lost its importance, buried by the emotions that terrified her.

Was she falling in love with this mountain man? The characters in her novels had never passed into real life. But now, as she thought of her heroine, wasn't it really her? She had never felt this way before—felt that she was actually her heroine and left wanting all of the things her heroine longed for. No, that wasn't true; her heroine had DONE all of the things Deedee longed to do.

She prepared for bed while the fire crackled. It must be one o'clock in the morning, and her legs were wobbly rubber bands because of the exhausting experience. Snuggling in the comfort of her bed with Cisco beside her, she fell into dreamless sleep, secure for the first time behind locked doors.

* * * * * *

Deedee heard Cisco's deep growl, and her eyes slipped open. The fire had died, but a pre-dawn light outlined the windows. She snapped on the bedside light, fearing the return of bears in the delusions of half sleep.

A naked man was teetering toward her, his drunkenness obvious. She screamed. Cisco jumped down from the bed and attacked the man's ankles, growling with rage. The man kicked Cisco aside and kept on coming. Yelping with pain, Cisco lay stunned.

When Deedee pulled her eyes from the naked pendulum, her scream intensified. She saw the lewd face. It was Greg. How had he gotten in? She remembered the spare key she had given him on the first day of constuction. God, how stupid of her not to demand its return.

Deedee jumped from the bed and backed up to the sliding door. He kept coming. "Get OUTTA HERE!!!" she screamed, tears of frustrated fear brimming from her eyes.

"Deedee, I just came to get my share of what you're passing around."

She pushed the door behind her. It caught in its track, leaving only a small opening. She squeezed out the narrow gap and ran to the banister, screaming, "E-e-e-ric, E-e-ric, HELP ME!!" When she tried to climb over to swing from the high parapet of the banister, Greg caught her arm and dragged her back to the house, back to the bed.

Recovering, Cisco attacked again. Greg grabbed the little dog by his collar, lifting him. Dragging Deedee along with his impetus, he threw the dog in the closet half of the bureau and snapped the door shut.

Turning, he ripped the cotton gown from Deedee and slavered at her bare breasts. He shoved her toward the bed and leaped on her as she bounced upward, pulling her hair to tip her head. Slobbering, his mouth came down on hers.

Freeing one of her hands from beneath his heavy body, Deedee raked his back with her nails. He flinched backward and slapped her hard across the face.

"You like it rough, Bitch?!"

Greg caught both her hands in one of his callused mitts and spread her legs with the other, aided by his knees.

Deedee bounced and thrashed. She gathered a wad in her mouth and spit in his face. Wiping the spit from his cheek, he smeared it over her areola and bent to lick it back off.

Deedee screamed in outrage and received another jarring slap. He mashed his scratchy face against her mouth and took her screams, moving himself into position.

The door crashed open—kicked by a mighty boot. Eric dropped the small shovel he was carrying and picked up the baseball bat that clattered to the floor at his storming entry.

Deedee whimpered when Greg released her mouth to stare at the thundering giant whose eyes promised pain.

Jumping up, Greg scrambled for the opening of the sliding door and escaped through it onto the patio. Eric's larger bulk would not fit through the narrow slot and he yelled as he impacted the door. It shivered and jolted upward. Finally, Eric hit the slatted floor of the patio, but too late. Greg had catapulted over the rail closest to the head of the hill and rolled, bumping and screaming in agony from the scratches to his bare skin, down the incline.

CHAPTER EIGHT

Eric heard her whimper again. He wanted to chase down the rapist and murder him. He would shove the ball bat up him, showing him how it felt to be violated. Instead, he sank to the bed beside Deedee. Her fragile beauty was exposed to his eyes, and he held his breath. A purple bruise was spreading across her cheek. He lifted her to him; her arms draped limply behind her.

"Deedee, oh, Deedee. My God, did he…?" He felt her shake her head.

"Noooo," she groaned, her voice raspy from screaming.

"I'll kill that filthy bastard!"

"No," she whispered. "It was my fault…what I said."

"Damn it, Woman. Why do you always think it's your fault?"

"How…how…?"

"How did I come so fast?" he finished for her. He continued as she nodded. "Big Dog passed away tonight. I was burying him out back when I heard your screams. Deedee, I saw him drag you from the balcony. I hated him for touching you, and I hated you for being with him."

"Big Dog…dead?" Deedee's chin began to quiver.

Eric watched as her eyes turned to crystals. Tears began to pool beneath her shimmering irises. Finally her silent tears flooded forth to trace a path to her lips. Eric embraced her and cried with her at the sharing of his sorrow.

"I d-don't c-care what you s-say, Eric. It's my fault. If I hadn't c-come to this mountain, Big Dog would st-still be alive."

Eric squeezed her tighter. He couldn't go on holding her naked body this way without replacing Greg in the rape. Cisco rescued him by crying plaintively from the closet.

When Eric moved to free the dog, Deedee pulled her grandmother's quilt around her body and rose. Cisco limped toward her, whining, and Deedee squatted on the floor beside him. Nothing seemed broken, but Cisco was shivering from the horrible experience. His shivering seemed to relieve Deedee of her own quaking because of her concern for her brave pet.

No more would Cisco cower behind the giant beast for protection or tumble from the bat of his huge paw. No more would he follow the big dog into the woods or roll on dead animals with him as if they were sweet perfume. How must Eric feel if she felt this loss so deeply? He was the one who needed her comfort, but all Deedee could think about was her own guilt. She looked up at him from the floor.

"I'm leaving, Eric…going back to Arizona. I've caused nothing but trouble for you since I've been here." Deedee looked back down at Cisco, unable to meet the hurt in his eyes. "I'll stay until the place is finished and put it up for sale. I'll give you first option on it to spare you another neighbor."

"Deedee, you haven't caused me trouble. You've brought life back to this mountain. You've been the delight of my life." Eric stared at his empty hands. He wanted to pull her back out of the blanket—crush her to him where she belonged.

"The bears, the pit, the cold, Poncho lost, Cisco injured, Big Dog dead, Greg and…and…Eric, I don't belong here. How many hints do I need to push me out? Hints, hell, they're hammer blows to my very existence!"

"Deedee, you're my life. Don't leave me. I have money. We'll go anywhere you want. I'll build you a castle if you ask it, just don't leave me." Eric's voice died in anguish.

"Eric, can't you see? Are you blind to what's happened? Every time you come near me, I tear you to pieces—cause you pain. Leave me alone, Eric. LEAVE ME ALONE!!!"

Deedee bowed her head over Cisco, rocking on the hard, board floor. She didn't see Eric's tortured look. She barely heard the door slip shut. Her heart was breaking into tiny shards from the deep loss she felt. The loss of Big Dog was only a small part of the piercing pain. She had found something here on this mountain that she had never possessed before. Freedom? Passion? Lust? She cried, and cried, and cried until the sun came to rest on her over-burdened shoulders.

* * * * * *

A strange, unsettling peace permeated the sounds of construction during the final days. The finishing touches were being put on the logs—a clear lacquer that let the knots and wood grain shine through, and the thick carpet was being laid in the bedroom. Men were hammering shingles on the roof.

Deedee didn't look for Eric nor search for him from her balcony. She poured her feelings into her computer. Possessed by the outpouring, she finished her novel in record time. All of her thoughts riveted to the mountain man, the book seemed to write itself.

Eric had taken her option and was buying her out. Everything was being handled through Mr. Breyer, so she didn't see the man who haunted her dreams and computer screen. It would be a dream come true if she could lay in his arms one last time, but she had caused him far too much damage. For his sake, she avoided him.

Eric had called the police, and an officer had come to see each of them. Rape cases were hard enough to prosecute; attempted rape nearly impossible. The fact that Deedee had given the man a key would be construed as consent by the defense lawyers. The officer promised to put an all-points bulletin out, but held little hope they would ever find Greg Thompson.

Activating her laser printer, Deedee went out onto the patio to wait for the book to run. Men were moving her bedroom suit into the new bedroom. She would be able to enjoy the finished addition on this last night, before she packed her trailer tomorrow. The contractor had met the deadline. He, himself, had supervised the final construction after what had happened with his foreman.

Deedee stared out over the hills. Her eyes were drawn down to the neighboring cabin.

He was there. His arms crossed in front of his chest, he mouthed, "I love you," and went in through his back door.

Heart pounding, Deedee continued to stare at the empty place where he had been. She had brought such misery to his life. How could he love her?

She supposed she loved him, too. No, she knew it for a fact. She had told him of her love in her book—had said all of the things she couldn't say to his face. How could she even speak to him when his eyes melted her into a puddle of hot jell-o?

It was best that she was leaving. He could go back to his isolated life, free of her constant harassment.

Her mind went over everything again. It all seemed so unreal, as if it had only happened to Penelope and not to her. At least she had followed Amy's advice. Deedee had done everything (almost) that she had written about. She wanted it to continue: the excitement, and turmoil, and sexual arousal that had kept her body and brain intensely stimulated since she came here. But, she couldn't go on hurting the hermit. She had invaded his domain with the naivet, of a school girl and had systematically begun to tear his world apart.

"I'm so sorry, Eric," she said through the emptiness that separated them.

Deedee had to put this experience behind her. She was ripping her heart to shreds by dwelling on him, thinking of his strong arms, his tongue, his manhood. Morbidly, Deedee turned and went back into HIS cabin. She could start her packing while she waited for the printer. Why dwell on things that might have been?

* * * * * * *

Eric watched in terror as the trailer was attached to her car and began to fill. It couldn't be happening. He had to prevent it somehow. The guts were being wrenched right out of him. He was fading into a pile of excrement, offal at her feet.

He had begged her not to leave him. She had given him life and was snatching it back away. Eric's pain became physical when he slammed his fist down on the solid coffee table. "Deedee, God, please don't leave me!" Eric put his injured hand against his eyes and poured out his pain. He hadn't cried like this since…since…

He couldn't watch her go. It would kill him to see her load her animals in the little car and drive away. Grabbing a wad of bills, still unspent, he waited until she climbed the hill and went to get in his jeep. He drove away—the pain of her leaving too great to bear.

Deedee pulled the door shut on the trailer and went back to collect Cisco and Poncho. Poncho was asleep, as usual, under the bed. Ironic that the little creature could stir up so much trouble and, yet, sleep through bears and rapes.

She locked the door to the lovely, little cabin and walked, reluctantly, to her car. Putting her pets inside, she looked toward his cabin. She couldn't leave without saying good-by. She had to thank him, one last time, for saving her life so often. Taking the key out of her purse, Deedee decided to use it as a ploy to see him. She had to leave him the key to what-was-now his cabin.

She walked across the turnaround and came to the tall grass around his house. Her heart was trying to jump out of her chest at the thought of seeing him, hearing his voice. Mounting his porch, she knocked on the formidable door. There was no answer; she turned the knob.

Entering, she said his name into the stillness, "Eric, Eric, are you here?" She looked in each room. When she saw his bed, she entered. Her picture was laying in its center, a well-read book beside it. Deedee let the book fall open to the sprain in the binding. The page was puckered from moisture. (His tears?)

Deedee reread the words she had written three years earlier. The words reminded her of their plight in the pit. Her hero and heroine were trapped in a storm cellar, a tornado raging across the Oklahoma plains. It was the female who required comfort; the female who quaked in fear and claustrophobia. Deedee read the chapter to its climax, a climax that she would never have.

How brutally their bodies had been torn apart by the flashing beams of light. How horrifying that she would never experience this blissful release with her mountain man.

Deedee went out into the blazing sun. How odd that on the day she was leaving the sun would finally warm this mountain. She went around the house to where Eric parked his jeep. The bare, worn ground was empty of the relic. A wooden cross caught her eye, and she was drawn to it. "BIG DOG" was etched into the dark wood. Tears sprang from Deedee's eyes to water the grave.

Seeing goldenrod growing nearby, she picked the sunny, golden spears and placed them on the grave. She had taken this wonderful animal from him. How could he ever forgive her for that? She had left a hole in his life that nothing could repair. Crying like a baby, she went to her car.

CHAPTER NINE

"Damn it, Amy, it just didn't work out!"

"He wants another date with you, Deedee. His exact words were, 'I think she's special. We really clicked.'"

"Yeah, clicked like a couple of pool balls."

"Deedee, you're just going to slip back into your same bad habits. It took me almost five months to get you out of this house. You can't backslide now."

"I just…Amy, I just…"

"You just what? What are you blithering about?"

"I'm just not ready to let a man maul me. This Greg Seever, of YOURS, spent twenty-five bucks for dinner and expected fifty bucks worth of servicing. Are all men like that these days?"

"You didn't? You did, Deedee."

"No, I didn't and don't intend to. Just his name gives me shivers. I never told you this, but I was very nearly raped by a man named Greg."

"You're kidding. In Colorado?"

"Yes, where else?"

"Deedee, you've never told me anything that happened to you up there. Is that the reason?"

Deedee thought of the many reasons she couldn't bring herself to talk about her trip. The major one was the love that she had found and lost. Painful memories were everpresent and were causing her to lose her career. Unable to think of anything else, she had not produced a single line toward a new novel that was viable.

"Read my book. It's mostly accurate." Deedee would let Amy believe everything that she had written. Maybe, then, she would stop bothering her by playing Cupid."It should be on the shelves by now. I've received my copies."

"Can't I have one of your copies?"

"Beggar! No, I need the support. Buy it just like everyone else."

"Ah, come on. You've got me wetting my pants to read it."

"Absolutely not. I'll go broke supporting your habit."

"Ahhhh, yes, Deedee, but what a lovely habit."

Amy left, hopefully to go to the book store. When her telephone rang, Deedee answered and accepted Greg's invitation for another evening out, lacking anything else of interest to do. Why not? Maybe, the little man would keep her mind off of…

Deedee was making it all right financially, but she had to sell Daniel's car and jewelry to make up for the loss she had taken on the cabin.

Eric had been more than generous with his offer. He had added his architectural fee to Deedee's asking price as he couldn't see making her pay for a plan that he would profit by. However, he didn't want her furnishings. Taking a loss on the rustic furniture couldn't be helped. Deedee had to leave them. She couldn't bring them back with her no matter how she longed to. They wouldn't have fit in.

She looked across the cold room. The brass and glass were rigid and unwelcoming against the stark, white plaster. The couch, its leather hot and bloody, seemed to be the only warmth in the whole room.

Deedee thought about selling. Not needing this much space, she thought of the cozy cabin, her grandmother's quilt finally hung on a rod on the wall, the warm, comfy fireplace, blazing against the cold, thin air. The quilt now lay in a drawer in her bedroom—out of place in this modern mausoleum.

The house next door had been put up for sale, and a sold sign went up the very next day. She could set her own asking price. Everyone was flocking to Arizona for their health. Deedee really didn't understand the procession. The scraggy land looked alien after the green on her mountain.

Her mountain? What a laugh. It was HIS mountain. All his now that she had run away in shame for what she had done to him. He had told her plainly on the day they met that he lived there because he didn't want company. He was a hermit. She was a trespasser.

Enough reminiscing. There was little time before Greg arrived to perform a little feminine magic on her lazy appearance.

The doorbell chimes startled her out of the daze she had fallen into gazing at her reflection. Moving nervously to the door, she offered entry to the clean-cut lawyer.

Again, as always, she made her comparisons to Eric. Greg was of shorter stature. His lean frame was muscled but must be described as wiry. A baby face glowed with a caring smile, which Deedee felt deceiving when he became amorous. Blond hair, shortly trimmed, and milky-blue eyes gave an illusion of the boy-next-door type.

Why had she consented when he called? Her life must, indeed, be an empty shell if she had to again endure his pawing. Well, it really was. Emptiness began, not when her husband died, but when she pulled away from a turnaround with a four-by-four trailer bouncing behind her car.

"Hi, Greg. Let me get my purse." Cisco and Poncho did not attack the man. How odd. Did they know something that she didn't? Should she trust her animals' judgement and leave this man alone as they had done? No, she mustn't. She was becoming a hermit just as surely as Eric. Was that why she had been so attracted to Eric? Was she basically a hermit?

Deedee tried to shed the disturbing thoughts as Greg held her wrap for her. She slipped backward into the jacket and thanked him. At least he was a gentleman in some things.

"I thought we could take in a movie tonight," he said as he opened her car door.

A dark theatre would be very convenient for his groping advances. "I had something like bowling in mind. Or, if you don't bowl, how about some pool. I'm a pretty good pool player for a female."

"Sorry, Deedee, I don't play pool, but bowling sounds good. If I can muster the energy. I've had a tedious day."

"Well, we can make a short evening of it if you're tired. I understand." Obviously, he didn't want to invest much time or money in someone who wasn't going to put out.

As they drove to the bowling alley, Greg initiated a conversation that surprised Deedee.

"Have you seen Amy lately?"

"Yes. She was over this afternoon. Apparently she's adamant about getting us together. I know I stay home much too much. Amy can't imagine that anyone would enjoy staying home." Deedee laughed, loosening the tension that was building between them. "Have you dated her, Greg?"

"No."

Had Deedee heard extreme disappointment in his voice?

"She must think we're made for each other. It was last July when she first mentioned you to me. Where did you meet her?" Deciding to explore this avenue, Deedee wondered how much Greg would disclose to her.

"We met through a case I was working on. I can't give you any details, but it was a long, drawn-out affair. We were on opposite sides of the issue, so it was awkward to ask her out, though I thought about it. Since then, we acknowledge each other in passing."

"So you're just acquaintances?"

"Yes."

Again, she heard the disappointment, but she didn't say anything further. They were pulling into the bowling alley, parking lot.

The crash and clunk of balls and the bellows of bawling, brawling men and women were soothing to Deedee. It was impossible to think, or remember, or feel sorry for herself amidst the cacophony of joyful bowlers. She and Greg didn't talk much while they waited for an open alley. Conversation had turned into a shouting match, so Deedee just sat and enjoyed the input. Grateful for this reminder that life went on, she relaxed and let her mind become a blur.

CHAPTER TEN

Eric held Deedee's novel in his hand. It had come direct from the publisher. He had managed to get his name on the priority mailing list by more connections. He peeled the brown paper away and saw a facsimile of himself and Deedee on the cover. Her hair was blond and his was black. The cover didn't interest him. Turning the book over, he found her face staring back at him.

This was a different Deedee than the one in his frame. This woman was younger, wiser. Her hair was loose over her shoulders instead of pulled back into a professional knot. He could swear she had worn the light blue, sweat suit for this picture. The picture, in black and white, didn't disguise the glimmering radiance of her hair. Eric touched the lips with his finger as if he could feel the pouting softness there.

"Deedee."

He sat on the couch to read by the winter sun. The snow was piled high around his unused jeep. His own fire outblazed that on the hearth as he cracked her book. The dedication slammed him to a halt. He knew Deedee had written these simple words with little thought, but Eric pulled a great deal of meaning from them. If only she could see what he saw, feel what he felt. It took him a long time to turn to the first page.

—For Eric and Big Dog, masters of the wild heart

Love, Deedee—

Eric became entrapped by the words. The sun faded, and he moved to the fireplace, throwing on another log. He sat before its light and kept reading.

When the bears came, Penelope and Roger made love on his bed. Her fear drove her into his arms and physical release. They made love a second time on HER destroyed bed while he comforted her for her lost pet.

When Eric climbed down the pit on a rope, it had come loose from the strain and had fallen in after him. They had made love and had risen to the heights in their passion and fear—climaxing with thunderbolts—before the men arrived to rescue them.

Big Dog (Samson) had lived through that horrendous night and had received a metal of heroism from the town's people. He lived, still, in her book and his beloved hills.

The rapist had succeeded in his attack against Penelope. Roger had captured the man and held him until the police arrived. He was now behind bars after the long trial—the trial that had caused Penelope so much pain. Roger had been there for her, to comfort and to testify. It took many long nights before she could accept him once more as her lover—the memories of rape too vivid and painful in her mind.

Only their deep love for one another had drawn them back into each other's arms in a storm of passion.

The book dripped with lust, love, wanting, caring, sharing, words for the future, words from the past. Her love for the hermit was laid bare before Eric. The words spilled from her mind—through these pages—to him. Her heart was opened like this book. Deedee was saying all of the things she hadn't said.

Eric reeled from her love. "God, Deedee, why did you leave?!" he growled in anger, relief, confusion, desire, and betrayal.

"It's only fiction—a story made up from some things that happened to her." Eric's voice startled him in the silent room. Not one word had passed his lips since the little car had disappeared from the turnaround. Reason told him to take her book lightly, to enjoy this work of fiction and then go on to another without giving it relevance. But, damn it, he didn't have the wherewithal to shrug off something that held his meaning for life. He could not revert back to the barbaric life he had led. She had opened him up. How could he, again, become Neanderthal Man?

He had gone to her cabin after she had left him so alone. It had charmed him; so perfect for her. Feeling lost from time, he touched the things she had touched. Eric had walked to the sink and remembered their hips bumping as they wrestled Cisco during his bath. Their arms had brushed, sending chills down his spine and quickening his loins.

She had left her bedding. It probably didn't match her decor in Tucson. Lifting the pillow, Eric had pressed his face into it. The smell of her hair was there—a smudge of lipstick from her lips, forever tilted into a smile like cardinal wings. He couldn't pull away. Sitting on her bed, he remembered her naked body. Freckles covered her like love buttons. He had wanted her so badly. God, how he wanted her still. It consumed every waking thought and every torturous dream.

It didn't matter what she said. This book proved her love. Her denial would no longer be tolerated. He would have her as surely as the sun would rise over this mountain.

Her fault! His pain! To hell with it. Nothing on God's Earth would keep him from her! Nothing!

Caught up in her fantasy, Eric read through to its conclusion before he could release the book long enough to sleep. A battle was raging in his dreams—a battle for life and love and Deedee—all one and the same thing.

CHAPTER ELEVEN

Deedee heard the moving van. "Wow! Already?!" She peered out the window and watched in envy as the moving men carried soft, suede couches and chairs into the house next door. Everything was made of heavy wood with overstuffed cushions. She frowned again at her frigid living room.

Cisco wanted out back. He was nearly tearing the door down in his demand. Looking out before she released him, Deedee saw a gangly puppy sniffing the fence. His whitetaped ears were threatening to get caught in the chain links. He was tan with a black muzzle. Even as a puppy, he was larger than Cisco.

Cisco tore toward him when Deedee finally opened the door. He seemed to go mad when he sniffed at the puppy. Cisco was leaping three feet off the ground.

"What in the world has gotten into you, Cisco?"

The two instant friends started running the fence line together in a new game of their own creation. Maybe Cisco was mellowing as he got older. She had never seen him so friendly with other animals until recently. Deedee would have to ask the neighbor if she could put Cisco over the fence to play once in a while.

She went back to her workroom to pound on her keyboard. This would be her third useless effort since she had written the book in Colorado so quickly. Having only been in Colorado two and a half weeks, she found it unbelievable what she had accomplished. For some reason her mind was blank each and every time she began a new plot.

What was wrong with her? What boggled her mind in midstream? She couldn't write the love scenes. Memories always flooded back of a "clean man" and a "big dog". How many times had she reached for him in her sleep? He was never there to fill her arms—only her dreams. Why had she fallen in love with a hermit? "Stupid, Deedee. Really stupid!"

This Greg Seever, she had gone out with, was laughable compared to Eric. He teetered on the edge of manhood. She had only dated him to shut Amy up. At least she would get a little relief from the constant pestering. Now, there was a block party planned. "You'll just HAVE to GO, Deedee. Just EVERYone will BE there." Deedee mocked Amy's syrupy voice.

Cisco was banging on the back door and running to the fence, banging and running. He obviously wanted her to come out to meet the new puppy. Of course she must. This was going to be a huge dog when he grew up. Maybe as big as Big Dog. Must she compare every living creature on Earth to Eric or Big Dog?

"What's your name?" she asked as if he could answer. "How cute you are. Ahhhh, did you get your ears cut? Poor thing."

Through the window panes, above the kitchen sink next door, a man was watching her.

Deedee had just finished the dinner dishes when Amy burst through her back door. "What are you doing coming in the back?"

"Oh, Deedee. God. You ought to see your neighbor. He's a dream, a hunk, a god. You have to introduce me."

"I don't know him, Amy. I've just met his dog."

"Don't you see? You can take something over to welcome him to the neighborhood. I could just happen to be with you. Do you have some cookies or something?"

"Geez, Amy, is sex all you ever think about?"

"Me??? That's all YOU ever write about! Oh, please, please! Do it for me. I've just got to meet him, Deedee. Ooooooooooo, he's so scrumptious."

"I swear, you're going to have to start paying back some of these favors. I'll do it on one condition."

"Anything. Oh, anything you ask."

"Do I note desperation in your voice. You've really got it bad."

"Deedee, you haven't seen him. My God, I could eat him up."

"Okay, okay. Promise you'll stop bugging me to go out all the time. If you'll do that, I'll take my peach cobbler over there."

"I promise. I swear."

Amy made crosses over her chest and even performed the Boy Scout sign for Deedee. Laughing, Deedee removed the cobbler from her fridge and put cellophane over it. It was a fitting welcome for a new neighbor. Deedee was no slouch when it came to homemade pie, and this one looked as scrumptious as Amy thought the man to be. She would be sorry for its loss when the hunger pangs of a sleepless midnight hour drove her to the kitchen.

Deedee and Amy strode up the perfectly-manicured sidewalk, Deedee carrying a casserole dish containing her offering. Amy had on a slinky, spaghetti-strapped dress, and Deedee wore a t-shirt and baggy sweatpants.

Amy rapped on the door, nearly breaking it down in her zealousness. Deedee and Amy both smiled up at the man who answered, but Deedee's smile froze. Since Deedee didn't speak or move for several minutes, Amy snatched the dish from her hands and offered it to the man.

"Hi, this is your new neighbor, Deedee, and I'm her friend Amy. Can we come in?"

Eric moved out of the way and swept them into the room with his arm. "I'm Eric Broddery. It's good to meet you, Amy, Deedee."

Literally dragging Deedee into the room, Amy continued to smile with oozing feminine appeal while Deedee stood and gawked at the man.

His beard was gone. His hair, a little shorter, was brushed behind his ears and locked into a pony tail. Deedee had never seen his square chin with the dimple in its center. His eyes held her as they always had, locked with his own, black, devil eyes. Her eyes didn't drop to his vested suit or his blue, striped tie until he released her to look at Amy.

Amy slithered toward him, and his eyes took her in. Jealousy broiled in Deedee's mind. She hated Amy. She hated Eric for being so damn good looking. She hated herself for not flying into his arms, to kiss the heartshaped mouth now exposed so brazenly to Amy's lusting eyes.

Eric held Amy's hands too long as he took the cobbler from her. "Thanks. It looks like I'll be very happy here with neighbors like you," he said.

"I'm sick!" Deedee pleaded and ran from the room, across the grass, and into her safe haven. She threw herself on the couch and cried. She was shaking when she ran to the bathroom to disgorge her rising dread. Hearing the front door open, she quickly washed her face and tried to quiet her tremors.

"Deedee. Deedee, where are you?" Amy called.

"I'm in the bathroom."

Amy burst in without invitation. "Oh, Deedee, you really were sick. I just thought that was a ploy to leave me alone with Eric. It worked. Thank you, Deedee. We have a date for the block party. Isn't that fantastic? Isn't he gorgeous?"

No wonder Cisco had gone crazy with the Great Dane puppy. Eric's smell was all over him. Was it a coincidence that the tables were turned, that she now had a trespasser in her life? Hardly. He was there for a purpose. Was it pay back time? Would she now be the recipient of total destruction to her life?

No one would ever believe her if she told them the man had been a hermit. He looked like he had just stepped out of the pages of a magazine, a model of perfect man.

He had asked her to marry him, once, in the throes of unspent passion. That was so long ago in a different world. Eric had invaded her world now. What did he want from her?

Deedee wouldn't go to the party. She wouldn't watch him kiss Amy. That's what he wanted—to torture Deedee as he and Amy rubbed together in a slow dance—kissed on the dance floor for all to see—for Deedee to see. Deedee wouldn't go to watch him destroy what was left of her sanity.

Her nerves were shattered. She knew that right now they were getting ready. Would he wear the black shirt and the cream suede suit? Would he put a carnation in his lapel and bring Amy a corsage? Would he kiss her as he pinned it to her bosom?

Earlier, Amy had begged Deedee to go to the block party. At least, now, she would keep her promise and not try to arrange another date. Damn Amy. She would have him in bed before the night was over. She would lie sated in his arms, replacing Deedee in an act that would never occur.

Even now, Deedee's body quivered at the thought of him, not as he was now but as he used to be. God, how she loved him. It was tearing her apart. She had come so close to dealing with her pain, and then, and then…

* * * * * *

"How do you like it?"

Deedee had opened the door to see Amy strutting in her latest creation of lewdity. The top was slit to her navel, covering only the areolas of her breasts. The skirt was tight to the point of strangulation and was split up her right side above the hip.

"God, Amy, you might as well go naked!" Deedee's face flushed, embarrassed by Amy's exhibitionism.

"It's perfect, don't you think? If this doesn't knock his eyes out, nothing will."

"You're right, Amy. It will. Go. Have fun."

"Aren't you coming? Deedee, this is the last party before New Years. You have to come."

"You promised," Deedee warned.

"Oh, sorry. Well, wish me luck."

"Luck." Deedee closed the door, crestfallen by Amy's appearance and what it would cause.

Walking out back, Deedee heard the roars of the party getting underway. The puppy whined for her attention, and she was drawn to the pathetic sound. Cisco was across the yard, indisposed at the moment, so the puppy was lonely.

Deedee rubbed behind the taped ears, and the pup squirmed in delight. Those cruel things, with wire holding them erect, must itch him horribly, but he would look beautiful and alert when he grew up. She couldn't imagine Eric doing this to an animal and felt certain that it had been done before Eric got the puppy. No, her Eric would leave the puppy as God had made him.

Her Eric? Amy's Eric. They were over there by now, in the midst of the noise and revelry. Hamburgers were sizzling on a grill; beer and booze were being passed around by bucket loads. The music started to blare on Deedee's nerves, and she went back into the house, leaving Cisco to take her place at the fence.

When she entered the living room, Poncho jumped out from under the chair, arching his back in a phony, threatening dance. Deedee picked him up and idly rubbed the side of his face, while Poncho yawed his jaw in pleasure. Switching on the television, she settled back to rest her mind. She hoped something could distract her from her dire imagination.

Hearing a knock at the door, she answered it, praying she didn't have to look at Amy's voluptuous display again. It was Greg Seever, dressed casually, with a drink in his hand.

"Deedee, why aren't you at the party?"

"I don't feel up to it."

"You do look a little down. Come on, Little Lady, you need some excitement to cheer you up."

"No. I'm sorry, Greg, but there's someone there I really don't want to see."

"It wouldn't be that Adonis that Amy's latched onto, would it?" Greg saw the visible flinch his words had caused Deedee; the undisguised pain in her eyes. Tears sprang to her eyes and she brushed at them ashamedly. He set his drink on the coffee table and drew her down on the couch to sit beside him. "Deedee, tell me about it. You have to talk to someone."

"Oh, he's just a character in my book."

"Is he the hermit?"

"Good heavens, Greg, how did you know about the hermit?"

"I've read your new book. Deedee, you're the queen of romance around here. Men have to read romances, nowadays, or they don't know what women expect of them."

"Is that why you were all over me the other night?"

"Hell, I thought that's what you wanted. You've really got it bad for this hermit guy, huh? Your eyes are as red as this couch."

"Yeah, I guess I do. He just moved here from Colorado, and when I saw him, all I could do was throw up."

"Christ, you do have it bad! I shouldn't have had to ask. I read the book."

"A lot of that was made up."

"And I'll bet a lot of it wasn't, Deedee."

"Why did he do this to me? Why did he move right next door to torture me like this?"

"More to the point, why the hell did you give him to Amy?!"

"What do you mean?"

"Man, Deedee, you're really dense. This hermit chases you down here, moves into the house next door, and you pawn him off on your friend?"

It did seem a little stupid of her, but Eric had wasted no time in asking Amy out.

"What business is this of yours, Greg?"

She didn't expect an answer to her hateful remark but got one anyway.

"I've got it just as bad for Amy. I've been hanging around, forever, trying to get her to pay some attention to me. She just keeps pawning me off, too. Well, you ought to know that since she pawned me off on you. After seeing her with that man tonight, I can understand why. She wants the perfect man, and I'm far from it."

"I didn't know. I suspected. Sorry, Greg, but Eric is hardly the perfect man, if that will make you feel any better."

"Well, sorry doesn't do anything. Sorry sits on the couch and lets the world go by."

"What would you do?!" Deedee lashed out at him. Hatred for her situation and dilemma forced her to find a target for her fury. "I can't bare to watch them together! It would rip the heart right out of me!"

Greg saw her face squinch up, and, instantly, more tears spilled from her eyes. He took her hand and spanked it like a naughty baby. "Cut it out! Deedee, straighten up! Think!"

"What do you mean 'Think!'? What good would that do?"

Greg laughed outright at her ludicrous statement. "God, Deedee, you of all people should know that 'thinking' is often the prelude to solving problems. What if this were happening to a heroine in your book? What would your heroine do? What would Penelope do if Roger went out with another woman?"

"She'd probably go out with another man. Two can play that game," she said defiantly.

"Bingo! I think you're more of a hermit than your hermit. Well, why are you hiding in your house, Penelope? Here's a man for you to go with, who is very anxious for you to get Amy off his arm."

"Didn't you see her, Greg? I could never compete with that. She was dripping sex when she left here."

"She doesn't have anything over you. You think those baggy clothes you wear hide what you have? God, no, Deedee. Baggy clothes have a way of bagging away from your body when you bend over to hand someone a drink. I'll guarantee you that you have three times the equipment Amy has!"

"Have you been looking down my top?!!"

"I'm a man. I've got eyes."

Deedee's fist automatically came up and socked him reprovingly on the arm. When she saw his little-boy pout, she burst into laughter.

"That's better," Greg said, laughing with her. "Now, get dressed. We have a party to break up. A very private party."

Deedee got up and headed for the bedroom.

"And wear baggy clothes," Greg added, grinning.

CHAPTER TWELVE

The party was in full swing when Deedee and Greg arrived arm in arm, smiling in conspiratorial pleasure. Amy eyeballed them and dragged Eric over to show him off, cooing and ahing at Deedee's unusual appearance.

"Wow, Deedee, are you trying to steal my thunder?" Amy commented when she saw Eric's eyes rivet to Deedee's perfect figure. Amy had always enjoyed having Deedee as a friend because she was no threat as far as men were concerned. But, now…

"How could I?" Deedee answered. Her dress was as modest as a schoolgirl's compared to Amy's. The soft gathers held her braless breasts decently concealed. The black fabric hugged the rest of her body to perfection, revealing her tiny waist and small shelf of a bottom. The strapless did expose the myriad freckles on her shoulders, but her coral curls helped to hide them.

Deedee avoided Eric's eyes. She couldn't afford to become a zombie in his gaze—not now, not before the scene was acted out. "Eric Broddery, this is Greg Seever. Eric is my new neighbor, Greg." Why not continue the charade that Eric had started? It was much easier to pretend she had no feeling whatsoever for this mountainous man with his deep timbred voice—so sexy.

The men shook hands, each knowing the other more than they wished.

"Are you all right, Deedee?" Eric asked. "Amy said you were sick."

The question, so many times asked, again failed to hear the truth. "I'm just fine. Something I ate." Deedee looked at Eric then, to see if he believed her. It was a mistake. He captured her with his black eyes—a butterfly thrashing in his net, struggling to get free.

Amy broke the spell by pulling Eric away, saying, "Come on, Eric. Let's find a table before they all fill up." She never took her hands off of him.

"Deedee, ARE you all right? You look green." Greg asked her pallid face as Amy and Eric moved out of earshot.

"Oh, God, Greg, don't ask me that! I'll never be all right again. Never!"

"Settle down. You're doing fine. Did you see the way he looked at you? Jesus, Deedee, I read about the way he devours you with his eyes, but I just thought you were waxing poetic. He really does."

"What are you blabbering about?"

"You must be blind as well as stupid. He loves you. I wish Amy looked at me with that raw hunger."

Not knowing whether to huff away for calling her stupid or thank him for pointing it out to her, she preferred to ignore the entire comment. "Greg, would you please get me a drink? A stiff one?"

"Sure."

Deedee stood like an island in the stream of happy revelers. She tried to avoid looking at Amy, trilling silly conversation into Eric's ear and pressing her exposed breast against his bare arm. Deedee seethed as Eric's eyes traveled down that front to Amy's naked navel, admiring on the way.

Then, they rose and began to dance to a slow tune. Deedee cringed but couldn't draw her eyes away from the undulating movement of their bodies. They moved as one, in a hypnotic rhythm, their hips meeting and rubbing. Damn Amy for being tall enough to feel his manhood pressed against her.

Crying out, Deedee instantly muffled the sound that had escaped her lips. She looked at the source of her pain—her hands. Her nails left indentations across her palms. She swore and crossed her arms in front of her, hoping she could somehow get through the rest of this evening in one piece.

Arriving back quickly with two drinks, Greg handed one to Deedee. She swigged it and handed Greg the empty glass. Taking the other one he held for himself, she downed it also.

"Oh no you don't. I'm not gonna stand here and watch you get smashed. If that's what you're planning, you can go back home and do it in your own house."

"Greg, if you'll remember, you're the one who dragged me over here. I was perfectly willing to stay in my house."

"Stiffen your backbone, Deedee, 'cause we're going in for the kill."

There were two empty chairs across the round patio table from Amy and Eric. Greg literally forced the stumbling Deedee over and plopped down in one, pulling her into the other. "Mind if we sit down?"

"Feel free," Amy warbled. "Deedee, you do look great tonight. What happened to the mousy housewife?"

The demeaning question infuriated Deedee. Is that how Amy saw her? A mousy housewife? Deedee made twice the pay that Amy did as a legal secretary, and not from being a mousy housewife.

"Do you want to dance, Amy?" Greg blurted, feeling Deedee's rising anger. Greg jumped up and pulled Amy to a standing position, peeling her away from Eric's arm. Deedee found herself alone with Eric. He rose from his chair and came to stand behind her. His large, warm hand came to rest on her bare shoulder and he leaned around her. His hot breath brushed her cheek, and she sucked in hers in a gasp.

"Deedee, dance with me."

It was not a question but demand. The gall of the man. How could he dare assume…? Deedee rose and turned in his arms, unwilling but unresisting. Like a robot, she assumed the position of the dutiful dance partner—habit or some unseen force taking over from her lack of will.

Eric's arms surrounded her, pinning her arms to her sides. All she could do was lift them to rest around his back. Crushing her against him, Eric engulfed her with his hands pressed firmly into the small of her back.

He nearly swooned from holding her familiar softness once more. Her breasts molded to the declivities in his chest and he could feel them become firmer from her arousal.

Pushing, Deedee tried to gain some distance from him to find her fragile composure, but he would not release her one iota from the prison of his arms. He started to move. She could feel his rising hardness against her stomach and mewed, unable to stop the helpless sound. She had to do or say something to halt her uncontrollable urges.

When Eric's hand came up to grasp her head and draw it toward his chest, she managed to distance her lower body from his. Too late, she was barely able to speak. "Why are you here?" she murmured into the knit of his shirt.

"Why were you there?"

"Eric, what are you doing in Tucson?" she persisted.

"I had a job, and I came to oversee it."

"That sounds like a lie."

Fingers intertwined with her hair, he pulled her away to look into her questing face. "Do you want it to be a lie?"

"Eric, quit bouncing my words back at me. You're driving me crazy."

"You don't think you've driven me crazy?" With this he pulled her back in to conform to his hard body.

Amy and Greg interrupted the answer that Deedee didn't have. When they wanted to change partners, Eric knew he couldn't refuse and still maintain the mystery of his relationship with Deedee. He stood facing her a few moments before he let her go to Greg's arms, using the time to bring his animal lust under control.

Fast music rescued him. He began to gyrate to the music, expecting Amy to follow. Amy hated the distance between them. She demured the dance, and asked to sit down. Reattaching herself to Eric's arm, she wriggled up against him. He let her.

Watching from poolside where Greg was keeping rhythm to the song, Deedee could take no more. "Greg," she said, "stay here and enjoy the party. I'm going home. My head is spinning. Too much to drink. I'm sorry."

"Are you going to be all right, Deedee?" Greg asked. His motive for asking was simply concern for her. He wanted to walk her home if she was that tipsy.

"Damn it!!" Deedee shrilled. "I never want to hear that BLASTED question again!!" She ran from the block party, escaping through the wooden gait that accessed the alley, leaving everyone staring after her in total befuddlement.

Before Greg saw Deedee disappear, Eric had clamped a large hand around his elbow.

"What happened?" Eric bellowed.

"I don't know what got into her. She said she had too much to drink and wanted to go home, then she just lost it."

Amy evaporated from Eric's mind as he pursued Deedee out of the fence. He looked down the alley but couldn't see her anywhere. "Deedee, are you here?"

Cowering behind a dumpster like a common criminal, Deedee felt deep shame. But she couldn't face him. She couldn't tear herself away from him again. Feeling like a naughty child, she continued to hide until Eric went back through the gate.

Once again her hose were ripped to shreds. Once again she had to brush weeds from her hair and grits of gravelly dirt from her knees. She knew she was a coward, but she had no choice. With no control over her lusting flesh, she would just have to avoid men. No, not men, just Eric.

But Eric had not gone back through the gate; he had gone back to close it to block out the sounds of the party. He heard the dry weeds snap and followed the sound. Before Deedee knew what was happening, she was being lifted bodily from her concealment. Eric shook her shoulders, slightly, to get her attention.

"Why are you hiding from me?" he stormed. "Do you think I would hurt you?"

"Leave me alone!"

"I've heard that before. You don't mean it, Deedee. Why don't you grow up and admit the truth to yourself."

Without waiting for her response, he lifted her off the ground and brought her lips to his with a crushing blow. She felt his teeth through her lower lip; the sharp edges threatening to cut her softer flesh.

His tongue broke through her resistence and took possession of her, body and soul. When Eric tore himself away from the demanding kiss, Deedee's body went limp in his supporting arms. She had fainted. (Swooned?) Whether from fear, illness, drink, or rapture, Eric couldn't tell. Lifting her up against his chest, he put his arm under her knees and began to carry her. From the bag strapped to her shoulder, he fished for her key after the one and a half block trip to her house. Cisco barked once but then recognized his friend with whining cries for attention.

Moving past the little dog, Eric took Deedee into her bedroom and placed her on the bed. He carefully began to remove her clothing. A small sound came from her lips at his jostling. A small sound came from his when he exposed her beautiful body. He went to her bureau to find a gown and dressed her. Surely she must have had too much to drink because she never opened her eyes throughout the painful ordeal. Drawing the covers over her, Eric turned away. It was the hardest thing he had ever done.

* * * * * *

"Where have you been?" Amy whined when he returned to sit beside her at the patio table.

"Someone had to make sure Deedee got home all right." Eric glared at Greg, his anger at Greg's failure to do so obvious. "She was very drunk."

"That was sweet of you, Eric. She's been acting awfully strange since she came back from Colorado. I'll be sure to tell her how gallant you were. She probably won't even remember. Drink affects her that way."

Amy squirmed up to Eric's arm as if nothing had interrupted her. Completely ignored, Greg left the couple to talk to some of his other friends he had seen at the party. His thoughts were not on Deedee or her drunken state. Now, as always, he watched Amy longingly and rubbed his injured arm.

The following morning, Eric answered his door. Amy was already in his living room, as usual, vamping him with every seduction known to woman. Eric hadn't discouraged her. If it took jealousy to bring Deedee back to her senses, he would use it to its full advantage.

"Greg, nice to see you again. Come in," Eric said, a trifle surprised at the visit by the man he had only met briefly, the man who had escorted Deedee to the party and had mauled her on a date, had abandoned her in a drunken state. He didn't know whether to slug him now or wait to see what he had in mind by coming into the bear's den.

"Is Amy here?"

"Why, yes, she is. Have you come to see her?"

"I've come to see both of you. There are some things we need to hash out."

Amy was more than upset by Greg's arrival. She had tried and failed many, many times to incite Eric to perform in bed. The bikini, she now wore with a see-through fishnet cover, couldn't help but make him lust for her, and Greg shows up to put a monkey wrench in her plans. "Hi Greg. What are you doing here?" she asked, none too cordially.

"I think it's about time we all had a talk about Deedee."

"Deedee?" Amy blurted. "Why would we three need to talk about Deedee? Is she sick again?"

Eric remained standing when Greg sat down—uninvited—beside Amy. Eric's expression solemn, he stared at Greg with renewed interest. "Yes, Greg, what about Deedee?"

Greg was momentarily stymied by the stealth in Eric's tone of voice and knew he was treading into dangerous territory. Walking on egg shells, he began. "Yeah she's sick, lovesick. Both of you are tearing her to pieces. Amy, you're supposed to be her friend." Greg braced himself for the next onslaught. "Eric, you're supposed to be in love with her."

"What?!" Amy shouted. "Greg, what the hell are you talking about. They hardly know each other."

Eric was stunned to silence by Greg's interference and waited before he spoke. He had to calm himself before he completely lost control and went into a rampage against this puny man.

"Have you read Deedee's new book?" Greg asked her into the silence.

"A little of it," Amy answered, wondering where this was leading.

Greg looked up at Eric. He was towering over Amy and him like a monolith. "Well, Eric is the hermit!"

"No," Amy denied.

Eric sank into a chair across from them. He didn't have any idea what Greg was doing, but his curiosity pinned him to the spot.

Greg had to steel his courage. Amy's presence as a witness made him a little braver. He wouldn't want to meet this man on a dark street corner. He wouldn't have wanted to follow Eric into the dark alley when he went after Deedee. "You're both making her miserable. Why? She deserves better. Eric, you loved her once."

"Once?!" Eric could no longer hold his anger. "You pompous little man, what do you know about how I feel? You just came here to get me out of the way so you can have her all to yourself."

"No, you're wrong, Eric. I came here to say…Amy, I love you. I've loved you since the day we met. Don't shove me off on someone else anymore. You're the only person I ever wanted—the only one I ever think about. Just because I'm not tall, dark, and handsome doesn't mean I can't make you happy. If you would give me half a chance, I promise you won't regret it."

Eric and Amy were both flabbergasted by Greg's little speech. So, this was the man's purpose in coming here, Eric thought. He wanted Amy. It had nothing to do with Deedee. He had just been using that as a ruse.

She took Greg's hand to console him. "Oh, Greg, I had no idea. I'm sorry, but I'm dating Eric right now. I really don't like to date more than one man at a time. I hope you understand."

"What?! Can't you see he's using you?" Greg urged. "He's just trying to make Deedee jealous. Good God, Amy, why do you think he moved all the way from Colorado to live right next door to Deedee? Do you think he just wanted her to introduce him to some of her sexy friends?" Greg roared in hysterical laughter.

Watching and waiting, Eric sat as an outside observer. Neither Greg nor Amy looked at him. They were involved in their own little drama. Eric no longer cared what they were saying. As they always had been and always would be, his thoughts were glued to Deedee. These two people were using his house as an arena for their little epic, which really had nothing to do with him.

Amy was horrified at what Greg was saying. Though many men had used her, she had never had to face the fact. "Why are you saying such things? They're nonsense. Deedee has never said anything about knowing Eric in Colorado. And, even if he is the man Deedee based her novel on, so what? She wrote romances the whole time she was happily married to Daniel. That doesn't mean she was in love with her characters."

Eric absorbed what she said even though he was trying to close his mind to them. It had a ring of familiarity to it. Was it something he had told himself? Amy was saying how ridiculous it was to believe Deedee truly felt everything she wrote. Even if Deedee didn't love him…

"Amy, I do love her. I wanted you here so I could find out everything you know about her. Maybe I've been fooling myself, but I believe she loves the hermit, and yes, I am the hermit."

"Well I'll be damned!" she leered at Eric. "You really were using me. How could you?"

Greg put his arm around her, taking advantage of her realization. "Come on, Amy, let's get out of here."

"Oh, no you don't!" Eric roared. "You said we're tearing Deedee to pieces. Explain!"

Looking into Eric's eyes, Greg had little choice. He would play the puppet as the mountain man pulled his strings. "That night of the block party, I went over to her house. She'd been crying a lot, and just the mention of you with Amy and she started up again. I told her she needed to go over there if she loved you so much, and I scolded her for letting Amy go with you in the first place.

"Well, it was a big mistake to go to the party. When she saw you with Amy, she downed two four-shot drinks like they were water, and then she had to sit there and watch Amy rub her tits all over you. Sorry, Amy, no offense. How do you think she felt, Eric? She loves you. Whatever you were trying to get revenge for—you've succeeded. I think that should even the score. Or, do you have further degradation in mind for her?"

Regardless of the pain and anger Greg's words had caused him, Eric knew that Greg was right. "I'm just a bumbling idiot when it comes to Deedee. Ten years of abject isolation didn't prepare me for this complicated game. Some of Deedee's books showed that jealousy would bring out hidden emotions. I never meant to hurt her. God, Greg, I love her. But, I don't know what to do to win her. I've tried. I've even begged, to no avail."

* * * * * * *

Amy was, for once, totally ignored while two men discussed her demure, reclusive friend. Amy couldn't understand all this folderol over plain old Deedee. Maybe there was a wildcat lurking behind that house-kitten exterior. Pacifying her ego, Amy consoled herself with the old saying 'For every heart a fire burns somewhere'. Apparently, Eric's fire didn't burn for her, but Greg was beginning to look like a powerful presence. She continued to sit quietly.

"Hey, I have a brilliant idea," Greg said, excited by his brainstorm. "Remember when you and Deedee were trapped in the pit? Did that really happen?"

"Yes."

"Are you really claustrophobic?"

"Yes."

"Eric, this might be pretty painful for you, but what if you were to arrange…"

CHAPTER THIRTEEN

As the days passed, Deedee stayed in slolitary confinement. When Amy called or came by, Deedee begged off, saying she was working and couldn't be disturbed. She paced her pristine prison, staring out of the windows for a single glance of the mountain man. On one sunny afternoon, she stood gawking from her kitchen window as he trained the puppy to obey commands. On another cool evening, she watched as Eric and Amy met on his front porch. She could not see them after they entered his house. His garage formed a baracade from her longing, starving eyes.

Last week-end at the block party, she had lost all memory of what happened after that kiss in the alley. Oblivious in his arms, she had literally lost consciousness. The next thing she knew, she was in her own bed. How had she gotten there? Embarrassment prevented her from asking Amy because jealousy also burned against her. Love knew no boundaries such as friendship or loyalties. When it came to her feelings for Eric, all else dwindled to insignificance.

Ironically, her writer's block had disappeared. Words were pouring forth onto her screen from deep wells within her. Was Eric's presence back in her life the reason for this? The evidence all pointed to that surmise. Would she have to stay with Eric in order to enjoy fruition of her work? That wasn't possible anymore. Not now.

So long ago, he had told her that she had brought life to his mountain. Maybe he had spoken the truth. He was no longer a hermit but was socializing and reacting like any normal American male—toward Amy. Deedee should be happy that she had helped him toward healing. If she truly loved him, she should be pleased that he was back into life—Amy's life.

On the night that Deedee was almost raped, she had tried to shut him from her mind and life. His anguished words came back to her now. He had said he hated her for being with Greg Thompson. Deedee had felt so soiled. Maybe Eric thought that she had led Greg on. Greg was there every day working on the cabin. Did Deedee say something or do something? Yes. She had shouted it to the rooftops. "I practice what I preach." She was lucky it wasn't a gang bang. All of the carpenters had heard her and seen her flaunting Eric's shirt over her nighty. All of them knew she was a romance writer. How many had read what she preached? The hermit had.

Why did she continue to think of him as the mountain man?—the hermit? He was a highly-respected architect, classic, professional in his appearance. Was it because she wanted to push him back into the past where no one threatened to take him away from her?—back to the mountain where she was the only woman and he was the only man?

Like a lightening strike to her brain, she knew that's exactly what she wanted. HE, SHE, THE MOUNTAIN. "Why, why, why Deedee did you ever leave him there? He begged you not to. Afraid you were causing him pain, you kill yourself? Stupid, Deedee, stupid."

Eric had called her the day after the party. Unequivocally, she had told him to leave her alone. Why must he keep torturing her? It had taken her so long to heal the wound she had received on that mountain. Now, he wanted to renew her deep feelings and start the hurt all over again. Why did he persist when she had made her meaning clear? He probably wondered the same thing about her. He had made his meaning clear on the very first day she had met him, yet she had persisted in getting in his way.

Cisco started jumping at the front door, frantically. The last time he did that, Poncho had slipped out the door. But Poncho was lying on the couch, safe and toasty. "Cisco, stop that!" Cisco merely ran to the window and peered out the crack his nose had made in the curtains. His feet scraped the top of the red leather. His whines turned into begging cries, growls, and then back into whines.

Deedee went to draw back the curtain. There was nothing there: no children, no people walking their dogs, no noisy jalopies or meter readers. Maybe the Dane puppy had gotten out. Deedee ran to the back to check the puppy and the gate to his yard.

The puppy was blapping the back door, crying for entry. Why didn't Eric let him in? The puppy was rarely made to suffer the heat of this Indian Summer. No shade sheltered him in the west yard.

Cisco was back at the front door, jumping and bounding at the barrier. There was only one way to find out what possessed him. She took his leash from the closet and hooked it to his rhinestone collar. He did three spins and ran under her legs. Deedee untangled him and opened the door.

Pulling and choking, Cisco dragged Deedee to Eric's house—Eric's front door. "Oh no, Cisco. You can't play with him now. Come on. Come on home."

Deedee yanked him from the porch while he backed and strained and shook and yelped against the restraint of the leash.

"God, what's wrong with you?"

Then she heard it, too—the banging, a whisper of pain. "Eric?" she asked the closed door. Cisco's panic spread to her, pumping through her brain and limbs. She tried the door, and it gave to her touch as it always had. "E-e-ric?"

* * * * * * *

Why had Eric agreed to this horrid plan. It was a last resort. Deedee had gone on with her life as if he never existed. How could she?

How could he? How could he live through this terror? He was suffocating. He would die in this closet of sheer terror.

No. Greg said he would come to check on him after dinner. How long was that? How long had he been here? Eric would wind up in a rubber room. Once again he was locked in a prison of his own making. His sanity was slipping away with every boom of his heart—every pound of his fist. He thought of Deedee. Deedee would have to rescue him—save him from his own lunacy and certain death.

He screamed her name with the last of his air and gasped. The air was gone from this tiny, tiny room. Eric began to pant. He couldn't breathe. Maybe Greg wouldn't come. Maybe Greg wanted him dead; then Greg could have

Deedee and Amy. Oh, God, why had he pulled this stupid stunt? He had the mental capacity of a five-year-old child.

Eric remembered Deedee lying in his arms, helpless, naked, and trembling after the attempted rape. If he had only taken her then, maybe she wouldn't have left him and none of this would be happening. He imagined he heard her voice speak his name, and he hit the door in agony and defeat.

"God, Deedee, you own my heart, my life, my love, and you're crushing them to cinders. You're killing me. If you could only love me."

Hearing his lament and another crash of fist to wood, she searched for him. When she ran into the hallway, Cisco tried to leap on the box that blocked her path. The closet door quaked as his fist hit it again.

It was obvious what had happened. Deedee straind to lift the heavy box that had fallen off the stack, and she tediously placed it back on the high pile. The box had apparently tilted off-balance while he unpacked the contents and had hit the door to lodge in place, imprisoning Eric in his hall closet.

Deedee opened the door and was shocked by what she saw. His face was ashen. Tears splattered his cheeks and shirt. Eric was hyperventilating, and blue tinged his pallid lips. Deedee traced her finger across his cold lips and pulled him toward the bed that stood in the room nearby.

Collapsing against the mattress, Eric sat trembling on the bed. He couldn't speak. His breath was coming in short spurts, choking him of life-giving oxygen to his blood. Deedee bent and pressed her breasts into his face, using them as one would use a paper bag, to restrict the gaping mouth and flaring nostrils. Gradually, his breathing slowed and his vibrating spasms ceased. He relaxed against her. She released him and sat down beside him on the bed, cooing soothing words into his ear.

Cisco had sat like a statue before them but landed in the middle of Eric's lap when Deedee gave him clearance.

"You owe your life to him, Eric," Deedee said of the demanding dog. "He wouldn't give up and forced me to come over here."

"Thank you, Cisco," Eric said, frisking the fuzzy Poodle hair with his large, gentle hands. "Thank you, too, Deedee. I...I..."

"I know. It must have been terrible for you. You should see a psychiatrist. Maybe one could help you get over your claustrophobia. It's a treatable condition."

"No. They can't remove the memories that tear at my mind. Deedee, I know why this happens and when it started. I want to tell you something I've never told anyone else in my life."

Eric held her hand tightly but turned away from her. He didn't want to see the flickering fear in her eyes. "It was thirteen years ago. Christine and I were newlyweds still, only married six months. We lived in the quiet of a North Dakota countryside, while she painted and I drew my plans.

"One night two men came with guns. They forced me into the closet, Deedee, while they...while they..."

"Eric, don't tell me if it's too painful for you."

"I must. You, of all people, have to know the truth. While I was locked in that closet, scream after scream after scream came from Christine. And from me. They were mutilating her—no rape—just carving her up to hear her scream. There are people like that, Deedee, people who find pleasure and eroticism in pain and gore.

"The screams had ceased, and they were gone by the time I had shredded the boards to release myself. I ran to her. She was…OH, GOD!!!"

Deedee braced him with her arms while he hung his head and cried. They sat quietly for long minutes before he could continue. Deedee didn't want him to continue. She didn't want to hear the rest. "Don't, Eric. Don't torture yourself like this."

"I called the police. Her blood was all over me. I was incoherent. The knife the murderers had used was the one from the kitchen I had used to carve the roast for dinner. I always helped her with little things like that.

"The police assumed we had had a violent fight. My fist was pulp from beating on the closet door. But they couldn't tell from which side of the door the blows had originated. Their was an equal amount of blood and splinters on the inside and outside. They believed I had vented my rage on the door and then it had escalated to the knife.

"The murderers had been very careful. They left no sign of their presence. I suffered through the trial in a daze. Everyone I knew turned against me. Even my own lawyer believed in my guilt.

"I spent two years in prison before the two men were caught in the act, in a repetition of the crime. They were in Nebraska. When they received the death penalty, they broke down and confessed to three other crimes. That just showed their stupidity. Appeals would have kept them alive and me in prison for many, many years.

"Of course, I was released, and the local newspapers professed my innocence. But it didn't stop the whispers. The lewd remarks from my ex-friends and ex-clients tormented me. You see, Deedee, everyone knows what goes on in prison. They automatically labeled me. No one would believe that I had abstained from sex completely during those two years in prison and all the years since."

All the years since? Deedee thought of the meaning of what that brief statement implied. He hadn't taken what Amy offered so implicitly.

"Oh, Eric, I'm so sorry. You've suffered long enough for something that happened so many years ago. Please, what can I do to help you?"

Eric leaned across her and pulled the book from the top of his nightstand. It was then that Deedee saw the eleven by fourteen, color portrait of herself that stood there also. How had he gotten it? This was not a picture torn from a book jacket, yet it was the pose used on her latest novel.

"Is this true?" Eric asked, referring to her book.

"You know it isn't, Eric. You were there."

"I don't mean the sex, Deedee. I mean the words. Are the words of love true? Who were you speaking your heart to when you wrote the words—fifty million strangers?"

When she wouldn't answer, Eric stared into her glimmering jewels. Her misting, topaz eyes melted into his. He lifted her chin with two fingers and pressed his lips to hers, gently, guiveringly.

He let her go and rose from the bed. Unsnapping Cisco's leash, he carried the little dog to his back door and put him out. The two dog buddies wagged in enthusiasm to finally be together and ran tumbling across the grass.

Eric went back to the bedroom. She was still there, sitting frozen on his bed. The mere fact that she was still there gave him leave to do what he must do. He pressed her backward and hovered over her; his hot breath intensifying her heated flesh.

"Deedee, how do you think I felt reading that book? Frustrated and alone on that mountain, Roger made love to the woman I love. Roger was consumed by your fire and sated as your flames licked at his arousal. I was unfulfilled with only an imaginary Penelope to satisfy my love for you. God, Deedee, Roger and Penelope are living happily ever after on their mountain. What happens to us? What happens to the pretense of OUR lives? Must we keep pretending? I want you, Deedee, not an illusion, not words on a page. YOU!!"

Deedee couldn't answer. Still locked in his eyes, her mouth opened in shock and wonder at his words. He descended on that open mouth, his tongue ravishing her with the passion he had kept locked away so long…so long.

Deedee's legs grew weak as she succumbed to his words and time-torn kiss. Eric was here for HER, not Amy. He had been unable to go on without her. He had come running to Tucson—to her. She had not caused him pain by being his neighbor and would-be lover on a mountain. She had caused him pain by leaving him there, by abandoning him to a life he could no longer tolerate.

Deedee moaned his name before his tongue plunged deeper into her soul. Placing his hand behind her back, he lifted her slight body up from the bed to press against his hardening pelvis. She roused at the impact, and her muscles shook from wanting him. He released her bra to expose her pale, freckled beauty.

Eric laid her gently down and held her eyes while he removed the remainder of her clothing. He bent to trace her freckles down to her belly, still tight and firm because of her childlessness. Gooseflesh arose over every pore when his thick hair brushed her breasts and then her stomach. His tongue tormented her and moved along her inner thigh, his breath hot against her golden hair.

Deedee reached for him, wanting desperately to feel his thrusting manhood. She tore at the clothing that prevented her from feeling him, feeling his rippling muscles while he explored her awakened eroticism, feeling the blood surging into his swollen manhead. Freeing the snap, she didn't take the time to undo the frustrating zipper. She pushed her slim hand down the length of his hard stomach and found the prize she was seeking.

Eric growled like an animal as she took him in her hot hand. Then he whispered, "God, Deedee, no. I want to be inside you."

Eric pulled her hand away and removed the barrier of his clothing, simultaneously sliding her shorts over her freckled toes.

Bare and willing, she pulled him toward her. He covered her mouth and sucked the breath from her lungs, leaving her gasping and clutching at his rising hips.

The sprawling legs finally opened for his benefit, and it was he instead of the black Poodle who lay within the thrashing limbs. They were his fingers instead of the ferret's that clasped her radiant hair as he tried to consume her in one final thrust.

The climax, too soon in coming, left Deedee moaning as she felt Eric soften within her. He lingered, kissing her eyebrows, and earlobes, and fluttering lashes, and tears of unsatisfied need. Deedee moaned a different moan as he engorged again, and she clung to him as he rolled to lay beneath her.

Eric wanted to see the woman he had pined for, longed for, would have killed for. She rode him like a bucking cowgirl while he relished her body and aroused her breasts. Eric reached upward to kiss that lovely mouth, to lick the tears that trickled to become entrapped in salty puddles at the corners of her lips "Marry me. Oh God, marry me, Deedee. I'll never release you from the prison of my love."

His answer waited for the mewling sounds that rose from deep within her. They rose in pitch and timbre to the rhythm of their want. Eric and Deedee swallowed each other to sate their hunger, and he rose with her up, up, up, into excruciating fullfillment and crashing back down again into a soft pile of pulsating, satisfied flesh.

Deedee broke into tears from the ecstasy of it and buried her head against his chest, and Eric held her close against some unseen enemy.

"Deedee, oh, Deedee, I'm so sorry I did this to you. You weren't ready. You pitied me. Are you all right?"

The question, so often asked, now pierced to the heart of her. Was she a child who skinned her knee? "How could you ask me that?" Deedee leaped from the crumpled bed and the nude mountain man, tears now streaming in ire. "How could anyone be all right after…after…" She hurried to gather her clothing and pulled them on. Carrying her shoes and bra, she fled from the room, the house, the man.

She slammed her door and fell onto the couch, still shaking in spasms. Her mind tried to sort the feelings, impossibly eluding her. Poncho crawled onto her lap and curled up on her bare legs. The bra and shoes fell from her hand. Finally her tremors slackened, her body relaxed as she pet the soft ball of fur. His musky odor rose up to her, comforting in its pungent scent.

All of her haunting dreams had been encompassed, revealed, and consummated on his bed. The dreams had not prepared her for the real thing. It had never been like that with Daniel. They had been more like a couple of old shoes—well-worn, comfortable, but lacking in polish and luster. Eric had ripped her heart out and laid it bare before her—exposed to be trampled at someone's will. Someone—HA—the hermit's will. How had she so completely lost control of her life? He could just look at her and she...she...My God, she was clay in his hands to be sculpted to his every desire. Where was Deedee—the dynamite author—the independent woman? Eric overwhelmed her, engulfed her in his gigantic shadow.

No sooner had her trembling, sated, mass of flesh stopped shuddering, when she heard a knock on the door. Eric stood there, his face a mask of disguised thoughts. He held Cisco in his hairy arms, the leash dangling, languidly, from his hand.

Embarrassment burned Deedee. She took Cisco from him and muttered her thanks.

Eric looked to her eyes, his eyes pleading her not to do this strange thing. The words that his eyes were saying did not pass from his lips.

"Mmmmmmm."

CHAPTER FOURTEEN

The throbbing cursor kept the beat of Deedee's ticking bomb of a brain. The novel that she had long sought was flowing onto the screen with a will of its own, a will that Deedee lacked.

He had done this to her. He had filled her mind with excitement, inticement, lurid words in the face of her pain. She couldn't stop. Like a bursting dam, she flooded her fresh, new disk.

Never ceasing until her pets could take no more, she would stop and nourish their small bodies with food while she nibbled at snacks. Nothing stopped the outpouring until she crashed her face into the keyboard in painful need of sleep.

This excess continued for three days to the exclusion of all else. Rubbing the aches in her neck and back, Deedee flicked on the television. She had to have some relief from her all-consuming obsession. It didn't work. The book continued to unfold in her mind and in her body.

Walking past the full-length mirror in her hallway, she halted in her tracks. That haggard woman couldn't be Deedee. Had she even neglected to brush her locks or wash her face. The blue mars under her eyes showed her, visibly, sheer exhaustion. Going to the bathroom, she poured herself a hot bubble-bath and stripped before another full-length mirror. At least her body had not shown the strain. She turned to admire her still-smiling cheeks. Not a bad rear end alignment for a gal her age.

A greenish-yellow stain captured her glance. Another beside it gave evidence to what it was. Eric had left his mark on her. After three days the bruise was lightening. She was glad she had not seen it in its full color. She felt like a branded animal. Why hadn't he just gone ahead and used a white-hot branding iron? Had she left similar signs of their passion on his body? Remembering her nails raking his shoulders, she thought it very likely. Why hadn't she continued to avoid mirrors? She didn't want to see her pain, nor did she want a reminder of her uncontrolled lust.

Sighing, she slipped beneath the snapping bubbles and leaned into the curve of the tub. Even if her mind would not rest, she could force her body to.

Soaking, Deedee let her mind wander away from her novel for the first time since Eric and she had made love. Her inspiration had not come from the mountains of Colorado for her last novel, it had come from the man of those mountains. Once again he had brought her the words to fill the pages. But what of the pages of life? What would fill those empty, barren pages?

She had quenched her passion in fire instead of water. The end result—it continued to burn. Her first novel in Eric's sight had been produced from the frustration of that passion. This second novel was born from the awe of fulfillment that still burned brightly in her mind. She had never known the actuality, so all of her previous novels had had the innocence of virginity in their naiveté,. The difference between Daniel and Eric was so profound that she would not doubt that Eric had ruptured her hymen— long hidden in obscurity throughout her sixteen-year marriage. Surely, that was not possible. Deedee giggled like a little girl at the silly thought.

The phone jangled when it rang on the nightstand mere inches from her tub. It had rung before. Let it. She would let nothing disturb her from this much deserved relaxation. If only the phone weren't so close and so persistent. On the tenth ring, she rose and wrapped a large towel around her dripping body.

"Hello!" she grumbled.

"Please don't hang up, Deedee. This is Eric. I have to talk to you, but you haven't been answering your phone or your door."

"That might have given a normal man a clue!"

"Please. I know you have a very good reason for leaving me in the lurch, so to speak. I don't want to pressure you, Deedee, just talk. Can't you spare me a fraction of your time? Would you let me take you out to dinner? Maybe a public place would make you feel more comfortable."

Eric was afraid to stop talking, afraid that he would hear the click in his ear that meant the end of the call. He didn't know what made this time different, but the click didn't peal the ring of doom into his ear. She was speaking. She was speaking with a civil tongue. There was still this one last chance.

"Okay. I owe you dinner, this time in my favorite restaurant. You've caught me in the shower. Give me one hour to dry and recoup some of my dignity."

Her choice of words disturbed him. Oddly, he took it as a personal offense. Deedee was accusing him of reducing her dignity somehow. If she only knew the high regard he held for her. Somehow he would show her and also earn her respect.

"Seven o'clock then? Thank you, Deedee. If you'll give me the name of the restaurant, I'll make our reservations."

"No!" Deedee heard her own irrational anger. What was she doing? He was only being courteous in trying to do her this favor. Had her independence threatened common, proper, human behavior? In a more refined voice, she recovered, "It's just that they know me so well there. It's a very busy establishment, Eric. We might not get in at this late hour unless I make the call."

"I'll bow to the hometown girl. Let me know if there's a complication. Thanks again, Deedee. I'll see you at seven."

With the last statement, Eric set the phone gently into its cradle and, uncharacteristically, broke into song. "Got a date with an angel, gonna meet her at seven…"

Answering Eric's knock, Deedee grinned in proud approval of her escort's appearance. If nothing else, she would be the envy of every single girl who saw them.

Eric, also, was unable to peel his eyes from the female perfection that faced him. No one could guess her age. If they ever came close from clues she trailed behind her, they would not believe the unbelievable. She was timeless like Sophia Loren or Elizabeth Taylor and just as beautiful. Or were his eyes the only ones that beheld her in this way? Was love really blind and was he caught in the darkness. He wouldn't mind going blind if she were the last vision he would see, to remember through all eternity.

Her pale-pastel-yellow suit, with blazer, matched the orange and yellow corsage he pinned to her lapel. Deedee blushed when she remembered the last pinning—an intimate moment that refused to leave her mind.

Eric was dressed in dark rust-colored suede with a yellow western shirt and bolo tie. He also wore western boots. Thank God he wasn't wearing the hat. She didn't understand what made mock cowboys so rude as to think they could wear a hat indoors without offending someone. A real cowboy removes his hat indoors, or used to, at any rate. Manners have flown out the window and have been replaced by so-called style. She was just showing her age and archaic rearing. Conventions changed but would Deedee?

She took the arm he offered and closed the door behind her. He opened the passenger door of the brand-spanking new jeep and lifted her into the high seat. Nervously, she straightened her jacket while she waited for him to get in.

When she looked up, her mouth came open. His house was a rainbow ablaze with bright Christmas colors. The entire roof line was blinking in happy rhythm while Santa Claus smiled and waved at her from the front lawn. How had she let Christmas creep so close without notice? She was delighted with Eric's industry.

Eric saw her radiant smile when he slipped into the bucket beside her. "I did this to please you, Deedee. I haven't put up decorations in...well, in a long while. Do you like it?"

"Yes, but if it's for me, why isn't it at my house?" she laughed.

"Only an oversight. I'll move it all tomorrow."

"Oh, Eric, I'm just kidding."

"I somehow knew that. I WILL help you put up your decorations, though, if you'll let me."

Starting up the jeep, Eric backed out of the drive and received directions from her to the restaurant. They were well down the residential road before Deedee answered him.

"Ordinarily, I would welcome a strong man to climb my ladder, but I think I ought to do it myself this year. I need the distraction from writing. I've felt very driven lately."

His favorite subject, Eric asked her about her new novel. He was not content with the general gist but wanted to know every detail she had written so far. With all of the rewrites this work would require, she was reluctant to divulge too much to him.

"I'm sorry, Eric. I can't tell you more. The work is still a mass of jumbled thoughts and it lacks coordination."

"That sounds a little like you, Deedee."

"How do you mean that?" she asked. Was he really saying what she thought he was saying, or was she misinterpreting him? It sounded like an insult.

"I'm just making small talk. Have you been writing continually since I saw you last, or has this book been in the works for a while? It sounds like you are pretty far along on it, yet you didn't mention it before now."

She couldn't tell him the truth—that she had had writer's block since she left Colorado and had not gotten rid of it until he arrived in Tucson. How would that sound? How would it affect a man's ego? How did it affect HER ego? Now, she had to face the awful truth—she could no longer function as a writer without this man in her life. That couldn't be true. There had to be another explanation.

"Oh, it's something that came to me. I don't recall how long it's been mulling in my mind. Sometimes it takes months for an idea to surface." That should be a safe reply. Deedee could go into politics if she cultivated these evasive answers.

"I'll want to read it. Do you have it titled?"

"Why, yes, I do. It's really a departure from my normal genré,. This will be a documentary, and it's titled 'Love, Life, or Lust'."

"'OR', Deedee? Are they noninclusive?"

She didn't know how to answer him. Eric was taxing her mind and tearing down every premise she had established with his tiny little question. Love and life could be inclusive, but could lust join them in any kind of unison. Obviously, Eric believed so. She had done little research on a very complicated subject. Challenged by him, she now knew her first serious work might as well go straight to the crematorium unless she took it more seriously.

Instead of answering, she sat with her hands in her lap and let the city blocks slide by in silence. Thinking and rethinking took the entire attention of her one-track mind. She felt him gently nudge her shoulder.

"We're here, Deedee. What have you been thinking about? It was as if you were no longer with me." He wanted to tell her how lonely that had made him feel, but decided not to. A red flag went up in his head followed by an amber. He would have to, at least, use caution in broaching the subject of his increasing (How could something so all-encompassing be increasing?) love for her.

"Sorry, I was preoccupied with my thoughts."

Eric shut off the engine and reached for her hand. She kept them hidden beneath the purse in her lap and smiled coyly at him.

"A penny for your thoughts?" he asked.

"Not for a million dollars, Eric. Shall we go in? I'm famished."

The restaurant was dimly lit when the maitre d' escorted them to a table privately secluded at the rear. This was not what Deedee had asked for but she had little choice with last minute reservations.

Eric was a perfect gentleman, pulling out her chair after asking if she wanted to remove her jacket. Prudishly, she kept the jacket on. Why should a little thing like that worry her? She convinced herself that it was because she didn't want to crush her corsage. Eric, however, removed his jacket and placed it over the back of his chair. Wishing he hadn't, Deedee stared at his muscles trying to burst through the thin cotton fabric.

"Okay, we're here," she said, attempting to allay her fears. "What did you want to talk to me about?"

"In time, Deedee. Let's just try to enjoy each other's company for a change. Every time I'm with you, all I do is put you on the spot. Would you like a cocktail before dinner?"

"Are you ordering coffee?"

"Yes, but don't let that stop you. I happen to prefer it."

"Oh, sure, I get plastered and lose all control while you have all of your faculties."

"Suit yourself. I'm not going to force alcohol down your throat so I can molest you. After all, I didn't touch you when I took you home from the block party, and you were quite plastered."

"What do you mean? You brought me home from the party? But…but…"

"Would you have preferred sleeping in the alley?"

"But, I was in bed. Did you put me to bed?"

"Yes. Why would that upset you? It's not as if I haven't seen you nude before. Don't you trust me after all we've been through together?"

"But that was before…"

The waiter interrupted to take their order. Deedee didn't mind because she needed time to think through this thing he had told her. What else was he keeping from her?

"Could you order for me, Deedee? I haven't had a chance to read the menu, and you're familiar with this place. Order me what you're having…with coffee."

After the order was given, the waiter hurried back to fill both of their cups with coffee. A devilish little smile curled Eric's lips as he watched her doctor hers with heavy cream and sugar. He relaxed against the back of his chair and waited for her to speak. She did not, nor even look at him.

"Deedee, why don't you look at my eyes when I talk to you? You look at my mouth, or shirt, or your hands. Do you find me so unattractive?"

How could she tell him that she got lost in his eyes? Could she explain how they melted her?—how she became a robot in his gaze? She still didn't look into his black eyes when she answered. "I don't know. I guess it's a nervous habit I developed out of shyness. You're very attractive, Eric, and I think you know that."

"No, I'm afraid I don't, but I'm glad you think so. You look beautiful, as always. Even in rags, you're beautiful."

"Have you seen me in rags?"

"Yes, as a matter of fact. In a hole, with grass in your hair and mud on your face. You were as lovely then as you are now. God, how I wanted you that night. I can't take my eyes off of you in any garb…or without."

"Getting back to the night of the party…when you undressed me and put me to bed. What else have you done that I'm not aware of, Eric?"

"I fear once again you were a damsel in distress, Deedee. I couldn't leave you there in that condition. I've told you this so many times, yet you refuse to believe me—I love you. I would never do anything to intentionally hurt you."

Deedee looked into his eyes, then, and saw the truth there. Now it was her turn for truth, but nothing came from her open mouth. Obstinate, she continued to balk at loving this man, or at least at letting him have that power over her. Knowing all of the reasons didn't help her when he trapped her like this. Thankfully, the tray arrived with two plates heaped with spaghetti; a meatball the size of a tennis ball topping each.

Eric grinned at the man-sized chunk of meat while the waiter continued to unload cheeses and breads onto their table. "Good grief. I'll bet no one leaves here hungry."

The waiter grinned. "No Sir." He poured fresh coffee in both of their cups and departed, ruining Deedee's carefully flavored coffee. She began anew to bring it back to that pale-brown color that she favored, trying to subdue the blush that was rising to her cheeks in the process.

A large bowl of chef's salad replaced the centerpiece, and Eric took the tongs, filling one of the empty, smaller bowls beside it. He handed the salad to Deedee.

"Thank you, Eric. I hope you don't mind salad during the meal. That's the way they do things here."

"Not at all," he answered, filling another and handing her the sprinkle cheese.

Even these simple courtesies surprised her. She had never been treated so special by anyone. There was little conversation as they enjoyed the enormous meal. Both had hearty appetites even with the turmoil between them. All Deedee could think about was the purpose of this meeting, and all Eric could think about was the woman who sat across from him, avoiding his eyes.

With only a few dregs of lettuce and two pieces of garlic bread left on the table, Eric folded his napkin and sat back to wait for her to finish. She squirmed from his silent scrutiny and quickly followed his example.

"Okay," she said as she laid down her napkin. "What did you want to talk about?"

"Deedee, haven't you heard anything I've said? I'm pleading with you to marry me. I can't live without you. I tried to forget the impact you had on my life, but it's just not possible." He leaned forward suddenly. "Marry me, Deedee."

Deedee was ogling his handsome face; her mouth agape in astonishment. Not understanding why his proposal shocked her, she, nonetheless, couldn't find any words. He rose and came around to stand beside her. She saw his body lowering to the floor as he knelt and took her left hand. A large marquis diamond slid onto her finger, and she pulled her eyes away from his to admire its brilliance.

"Please, my Love, will you marry me?" he concluded as he lifted her chin to meet his adoring eyes.

"Good God! I...I...don't know what to say. You ARE serious. I have to think. Let me think."

"Whatever your decision, the ring is yours, Deedee. "Eric kissed her hand and rose from the floor. He stepped to his chair and put on his jacket, concealing his deep disappointment from her. "Shall we go?" he asked, ready to assist her from her chair.

She followed him to the register after he had placed a generous tip on the table. Tripping over her own feet, she couldn't take her eyes off of the ring shining with a light of its own. It was her treat, but she forgot to pay because her thoughts were galloping elsewhere.

When they were well on their way, Deedee glanced out the window. "Where are we going? This isn't the way home."

"I want to show you something."

Fifteen minutes passed, and they pulled into a muddy lot with a mammoth steel and glass structure towering above them. Eric came around to help Deedee down from the jeep. "This is what I wanted to show you. Do you like it? It's my design."

The full moon reflected blue and gleaming from the portion of the building that was nearing completion. The remainder looked eerily like the skeleton of a huge dinosaur.

"It's BIG!"

"Are you afraid of heights?" Eric queried.

"How high?"

"It's only twenty stories. Not exactly the Empire State Building, but it's the largest I've done so far."

"Do you mean you want to take me up there somewhere?" she asked, pointing to the illusion of solidity.

Eric firmly took her hand and led her to a metal box. An accordion gate closed them off, and they began to ascend. Deedee inched closer to Eric while the lights of the city spanned farther and farther away from her until they began to disappear beneath the edge of the elevator.

A gust of wind rattled their tiny cage, and Deedee shivered. A strong arm came around her, instantly, to protect and support her. "It's quite safe, Love. You ought to see the three hundred pound foreman who uses this thing fifty times a day."

Slowly grinding, the elevator stopped, and Eric pulled back a second gate facing the building. He exited and tried to entice Deedee to follow. The floor she tippy-toed out onto was constructed of loose boards shoved up together. Though she was sure it was safe, it still wobbled at her slight weight.

When she was able to remove her eyes from her tedious footing, she gasped aloud at the panorama that expanded before her. Tucson's residential street lights, far in the distance, faded, turned to stars, and climbed the sky to diminish toward the brightness of the dazzling moon. There was nothing between Deedee and this vista except the metal beams of the construction.

She swiveled, wanting to see it all, and saw, instead, Eric holding a chair for her behind a table. It was only a card table but was covered with a linen table cloth. Two crystal goblets glittered by the light of the candle that stirred in the updraft from the city far below. A champagne bucket stood beside the table with a towel-wrapped, glass neck protruding from the ice it contained.

"Oh, Eric, what have you done?"

"It was meant to be a celebration if you said yes, Deedee. Now, we're just going to celebrate being together once again. Nothing could make me happier than being with you."

"I'm so sorry. I've ruined everything for you by my indecision. Can you ever forgive me?"

"Damn it, Deedee. There's nothing to forgive. There never has been. Please come and sit down."

Though she heard anger in his voice, his face was pleading with her. She went to the chair he proffered and sat down. He crossed to the side with the champagne and made an elaborate scene of popping the cork. Neither of them saw where the exploding cork went. Maybe someone would find it embedded in a steel girder like a rivet.

She took the glass he offered and held it until he poured his own. He sat down across from her.

"A toast, Deedee. To a mountain that longs for your return."

"That's not fair. Let me propose a toast. To the memory of Big Dog whose heart was bigger than that mountain."

"I'll drink to that."

Their glasses clinked, and they drank the tickling champagne, remembering another time, another place.

* * * * * * *

The jeep pulled into Eric's drive. Eric reached across the space that separated the bucket seats and pulled Deedee toward him. He kissed her softly and backed away. After seeing her lashes flutter in rapture, he took her more deeply into the abyss into which she was falling. Her breath was coming in short gasps, and he buried his face in her hair, smelling its sweet fragrance and feeling its silken tickle against his nose.

"Come inside with me, Deedee. I need you desperately."

She had never had a more incredible evening in all of her life. Everything had been so much more than perfect. Hesitantly, she tried to utter the minute thoughts that were causing her to resist him. It would be so easy to fall into bed with him and experience Heaven again. Her other persona rose to refuse him.

"I mustn't, Eric. You've given me so much to think about. My brain is a jumble. It wouldn't be fair to persuade me with your lovemaking. I can't be rational nor make a decision to your wonderful question with something like that distracting me."

He didn't say anything more. Moving around the car, he helped her down and walked her to her door. When she pressed the key into the lock, he stopped her hand before the lock clicked. "I don't understand you're reluctance. All I can do is love you and hope that you can find it in your heart to return that love in kind. Sleep with me close to your heart."

He bent to kiss her good-night. Unlike the deep passion that usually flowed between them, this kiss was fleeting—a gentle brush of tenderness.

Holding her lips with her fingers, Deedee turned the key as Eric walked away.

CHAPTER FIFTEEN

For the first time in many, many months, Deedee slept a dreamless sleep. Maybe it was from burnout, but on this one night, her mind was at peace. Awakening refreshed, she heard the telephone ring. She didn't answer it. Ten minutes later someone knocked at the door. She didn't answer it. Nor did she peer out of the window to see the departing person who had awaited her attention.

The heavy ring weighting down her finger brought her back to reality. The cool dawn of reason had to bring some answers to her questions. But she didn't want those answers in her present condition. She wanted to drift on the sea of oblivion that was currently giving her such relief.

After eating a bowl of cereal and letting Cisco escape to the backyard, Deedee went to her computer and pulled up "Love, Life, or Lust". She purposely reformatted the disk, the subject too heavy for her state of mind. She would go back to the lighthearted romance that she had started.

Had she decided what to tell Eric? No. There had to be some reason that she refused to think about it. Noon came and went. Not knowing or understanding why, she crawled into the attic and pulled down Daniel's elaborate Christmas decorations. Taking them into the garage, Deedee took down the ladder.

It was only nine days til Christmas. They say that the holidays can bring on deep depressions long left submerged. Was that what was happening to her? Each of the items she layed out held memories of Daniel. Those memories were of a life where her feelings and ambitions had been suppressed under the shadow of Daniel's.

He had tolerated her writing because of the money it generated. She never had to ask him for money when she wanted to indulge a whim. How convenient for him. But he had hated every minute she spent at her computer or doing research. He simply hadn't thought it was important.

Of course HIS work WAS important. She would listen for hours while he bragged of his great accomplishments. Those that she had made were not discussed. She had to pat her own back because Daniel would not. Now, who would remember his achievements? Ten years from now, he would be forgotten by all but her. One hundred years from now, maybe someone would find a dusty old book on a shelf in a library that would have her name on it. In this way she had surpassed Daniel, she had won a small piece of immortality.

Eric's strength of character was far greater than Daniel's. And his immortality had also been established in the art of his work. But would she now become his underling, his robot, his slave? Formidable and overwhelming, he would be much more oppressing than Daniel ever was.

She hit the garage door opener and carried the wooden sleigh to the front yard. After going back for the ladder, she placed it up against the one-story roof. Why not start with the heaviest and work her way down? Though the sleigh was cumbersome, it wasn't really too heavy for her to manage. She started up the ladder and made it to the fifth rung when she felt two strong hands clamp her hips.

"Deedee, come down from there. You're going to hurt yourself."

It was Eric. She should have known he would be lurking close by, just waiting for his chance to see her. "No. I'm fine."

He didn't release her hips until she humphed down the ladder. "Eric, I told you I wanted to do this myself."

"God, Deedee, I didn't know you were going to be carrying all this up to the roof. Be reasonable, will you?"

"It's always been on the roof. Maybe your Santa lands on the lawn, but mine lands on the roof." She faced him down with her hands on her hips, replacing his.

He persisted and insisted until she gave in to him. Didn't that prove, exactly, what she had been thinking about him? Climbing the ladder in her stead, Eric reached the top rung with the sleigh and shoved it up onto the roof to make room for him to follow.

Deedee shouted to him, "It goes ten paces from the chimney facing away from it!"

Eric turned to acknowledge her instructions, and, just then, a gust of wind caught the edge of the sleigh and lifted it toward him. It smacked him backward with enough force to send him off balance as he struggled to control the flapping piece of wood and the tilting ladder.

With eyes wide and mouth opening in a silent scream, all Deedee could do was watch when the ladder careened away from the house and teetered in mid-air before she could reach it. Hanging on for dear life, she tried to push the ladder back toward the house. Eric's weight had already taken it past the point of no return. He was still hanging onto the sleigh as if to protect it. Then with the slowness of eternity, the ladder came down on top of Eric's thudding body and clattered to the lawn with shards of broken plywood.

She heard the wind gush from his lungs. Running the length of the ladder, she nearly fell on his inanimate body. His eyes were open and so was his mouth, but he couldn't talk nor breathe. Deedee could only stare at the shocked eyes and wait for breath to return to the empty lungs. Relief finally came when he gasped and then groaned.

"Oh my God, Eric, are you all right?"

"My leg. Get help, Deedee. I think it's broken."

She looked where he pointed. The leg was lying at a peculiar angle, and there was blood seeping into the fabric of his pants. "Oh no! I'm so sorry, Eric. Don't move. I'll call."

Cisco tried to leap up her leg while she dialed the number. Ignoring him, she told the calm voice on the other end what had happened and was assured that someone was on the way. Struggling to get back out of the door without Cisco, she returned to sit on the grass beside Eric. Holding hands, they waited for the screaming siren.

X-rays showed compound fracture of the fibula and tibia. If that wasn't bad enough, the broken ankle on the other leg was more than enough to cripple Eric for at least three months if he was lucky.

Deedee stayed with him in the emergency room and the x-ray room and back to the emergency room. She couldn't stay with him when he was taken into surgery, but she was waiting in his assigned room when they brought him in and strapped him up into leg slings. Groggy and wearing a silly smile, Eric reached for her and giggled.

"Lie still, for Pete's sake."

As if in obedience, he closed his lids and fell fast asleep.

A nurse patted Deedee's arm, drawing her attention away from the sleeping mountain man. "Are you his wife?" the nurse asked sympathetically.

"No. We're just neighbors." She didn't know why she disclaimed him in such a way. Ashamed, she added, "He's asked me to marry him, however."

"Oh, I see. Well, he's going to sleep for at least four hours before the drugs begin to wear off. It's not necessary for you to stay unless you wish to."

"I do intend to stay. I have to be here when he wakes up."

"Yes, of course." Having done her duty, the nurse went about her various tasks of sticking needles into Eric and starting an IV.

Deedee couldn't believe he slept through it. The nurse poked him three times and then brought in fresh recruits to try. Soon the room was empty save for her and Eric. She scooted her stiff chair over to his bedside and held his hand, and there he found her when he awoke four hours later.

Pain had replaced the silly, drug-induced smile that he had greeted her with earlier. Deedee leaned over him and rubbed the wild hair from his forehead.

"The doctor was in, Eric. He said he would return tonight. This was all my fault. I don't know why I let you climb up there to begin with."

"For Christ's sake, Deedee, why does every single thing that happens have to be your fault? I don't think you're big enough to force me up a ladder." He flinched from the sharp pain that ran up his spine from the strain of his anguish. Forced into silence, he lay his head back on the pillow.

She wanted to say she was sorry for causing this recent agony but was afraid to. "Eric, you have to be still. Just listen to me. You're going to be laid up for quite some time. I've had several hours to do some thinking. Come and stay with me. I can move my office into the living room and give you the spare bedroom."

"No, Deedee. I couldn't put you out like that. I can hire someone to take care of me."

As if she hadn't heard him, she continued, "With your strong arms and a wheel chair, we should be able to manage just fine without your having to hire someone. God, Eric, it's the least I can do for you after all the times you've rescued me from my own stupidity."

"You don't owe me anything. If you do owe me something, it's only an answer to a guestion that I asked last night."

"I don't have that answer. I wish I did. Everything is happening so fast. That can wait. Right now we need to get you well. Don't worry about the money; my insurance should cover everything since you were injured on my property."

"The money isn't important. Don't even bother with it. Leave me alone for a little while, Deedee. I'm in a great deal of pain, and I can't hold this brave façade much longer."

"I understand. Of course you're in pain and here I am rattling away. I'll send the nurse in. Surely they have something for the pain. Hang in there." Kissing him on the top of his forehead, she picked up her things and left.

Eric's eyes rolled back in his head. The pain in his mind overcame the pain in his leg as he tried to sort out this complicated lady.

During Eric's six day stay in the hospital, nothing more was said about his proposal. Deedee came cheerily into his room several times a day bearing flowers, or candy, or books. They were not her books; he didn't read them.

He accepted her offer for care. There was more than one way to skin a cat, or so they say. Why would he refuse her generous offer to move in with her?

Everything had been prepared for him by the time the ambulence delivered him to her residence. Deedee had rented a hospital bed, with a trapeze, and a wheelchair, and had even gone to the trouble of having a ramp built to access her three step porch. By using his key, she had brought the things he would need from his house to do his work. His puppy played happily in her backyard with Cisco and was growing by leaps and bounds.

Things could have been better, however. Eric would prefer not being a completely helpless invalid, totally dependent on her caring administrations. Not exactly the honeymoon he had dreamed of.

On Christmas Eve, he sat in his wheelchair, handing her pretty bulbs while she placed them on the tree. They laughed together when she darkened the room and turned on the blinking lights. The exterior of her house remained dark as she had never had the heart (courage?) to use the ladder after his fall.

Deedee picked up the lone present that mysteriously appeared beneath the prickly branches and carried it to Eric's lap.

"What's this? You didn't have to buy me a gift, Deedee."

"Oh stop being so stubborn for a change and open it."

He peeled back the paper and lifted the lid on the large box. Lifting a handsome cowboy hat from the tissue paper, Eric smiled broadly. "Thank you, Deedee. I've always wanted one and never had the gumption to buy one for myself.”

“Well, I know you have the clothes to go with it.”

Eric pulled a small box from the sash of his robe. “I have something for you, too.”

“But how? You’ve been couped up in this house for a week.”

“I ordered it some time ago, and Amy brought it by the other day when you were shopping for the ham.”

“Amy?!” Jealousy pinched her mind, but his face looked so innocent and sincere that she suppressed it quickly. Taking the small present from his hand, she carefully removed the bow and foil wrapping. “Uhhhhhhhh,” she gasped as she lifted the paved, diamond heart from the cotton.

“Oh, Eric, I couldn’t accept this. It’s too extravagant.”

“If you must have a reason, Deedee, consider it payment for room, and board, and tender, loving care, even though I ordered it long before I took that plunge.”

“You had Amy over here when I wasn’t home?” Deedee let her imagination soar. “How could you after what you two…?”

“Good God, Deedee, Amy is your friend. Have you so little faith in me? If it weren’t for her and Greg I would have never made love to you the one and only time that I did!”

“What do you mean?! What did Amy have to do with it?!”

Now he had done it. He had stuck his big foot in his bigger mouth. “It’s not important.”

“Oh it’s not? Another one of your secret conspiracies?” She put the heart back in the box and put it in his lap. “I don't like secrets and conspiracies. How can you expect me to blindly trust you when I feel like I'm being manipulated all the time?"

"Okay. I'll come clean, but you're not going to like this."

As she sat across from him, listening with a bleak expression, he told her about Greg's visit and disclosure, of the plot to lock him in the closet and have Deedee rescue him. "I may have gone in there on purpose, Deedee," he concluded, "but my pain was not faked."

Incredulous at how naive and vulnerable she really was, she lashed out at him. Her placid face turned to one of rage and betrayal. The blinking tree was forgotten. The presents were forgotten. The whole blinking holiday was forgotten. "It was so easy, wasn't it? So easy to fool stupid Deedee. How Amy must have enjoyed that. And, Greg, I can hardly believe it about Greg. He seemed to really care how I felt. Oh, but no, they wouldn't care about stupid Deedee, helpless, stupid Deedee. 'Let's all help Eric make an ass of her. Let's all help Eric get her into bed so he can show her his sexual prowess.' Damn you to hell, Eric, and take my so-called friends with you!"

She stormed out of the room but came back. A diamond ring landed in Eric's lap beside the heart. He now held both of the symbols of his love while her bedroom door slammed behind him. Tears slid down his cheeks as he struggled to back the wheelchair to her door.

"Deedee, God I'm sorry. I would give my life to do it all over and somehow make it right. Let me in. I love you. Please don't shut me out."

There was no response. Eric went to his room and made ready for bed. Not to sleep. He knew the impossibility of that all too well.

The next morning, Deedee brought him his breakfast and placed the tray across his lap without a word. Going back to the kitchen, she began the morning-long job of preparing Christmas dinner. She worked like an automaton, taking the pies out of the oven and shoving the ham and pineapples in. She wasn't about to let all of this food waste away because she had been such a dupe.

As she cooked, she wracked her brain. Eric was helpless. She had offered to help him. Could she withdraw that offer because he had been truthful and told her of her own stupidity? No. She might be a dupe, but she was not cold-hearted.

During a break in her buzzing activity, she went to his room and stated bluntly. "I have some financial need right now, Eric. I would appreciate it if you would pay me whatever amount is appropriate for your care. I certainly won't put you out." She left before he could answer, as if there could be no choice for him.

"Merry Christmas," Eric muttered when he heard her rattle a pot in the kitchen. He hadn't planned to stay. There was no way he could make arrangements on Christmas Day to move out, but he had planned on leaving tomorrow. Sure, it had been wrong to trick her like that, but he had had the best of intentions. He would feel more guilty if he had just been using her, but he wanted to spend his whole life trying, impossibly, to make her happy.

How could he leave now? She needed money, and he could provide it. She wouldn't take it if he just gave it to her. Life would be hell for a while, but he had to stay to help her out. Damn, why did he keep blundering into these situations? Why did he have to be so truthful? She hadn't even asked; he had blurted out the whole story on his own volition. But would he rather she hear it from Greg or Amy?

As with Christmas Day, the following week was spent for Eric, in his room, within a house filled with polite sterility. Many times he wanted to scream just to hear something other than prim civilities, such as, "Thank you", "Yes, please" and "No, thank you".

On New Year's Eve Day, Deedee came to his room. "Eric, I wanted to inform you that I will be going out this evening. I've finished my manuscript, and Greg asked to take me to a New Year's party. I deserve to celebrate. Do you need someone to be here while I'm gone?"

Eventually he was able to stop gritting his teeth long enough to answer her. "No. I'll be fine."

Apparently things hadn't worked out for Greg and Amy. Eric wished that they had. He heard Deedee getting ready after he was brought his dinner. Thank God she didn't come to his room to show off how she looked. Hearing Greg's voice after the doorbell rang, he knew it was all over. How was he going to be able to lie here silently while she tore him to pieces, bit by bit?

At least she had finished her book. Anxiously, he got into his wheelchair and maneuvered into the next room. Her desk was set up back to back with his bed. He had heard her whacking away hour on hour while he stewed.

Keying up her menu, he found a likely prospect and brought it up. "Summer Dreams" was the title, and it promised to reveal her feelings after the summer she spent on a mountain.

He was doing it again. Hadn't he learned his lesson? Shutting off the computer, Eric returned to his room. Why did he continue to prowl behind her back? Oh, how he wanted to read her book, but this was not the way to go about it. Why didn't he just ask her?

Lights out and eyes staring at the dark ceiling, he heard her come in at two a.m. "Happy New Year, Deedee," he said when her footsteps entered the hall.

"Happy New Year, Eric. Do you need a sleeping pill?"

"No thank you. Good night."

"Good night."

* * * * * * *

The next morning when breakfast arrived, he got up the courage to do things properly. "May I read your new book, Deedee. You know I'm a fan."

"I would rather you didn't."

"Have pity." Manipulating again, are we? "I don't have anything else to do," he pleaded.

"Oh, all right. I guess you'll read it sooner or later, anyway. I'll make a copy before I mail it."

"Thank you. You won't be sorry."

What a stupid thing for him to say after jumping down her throat everytime she said she was sorry. Why didn't he just throw it up in her face? When she came back for his tray, he would beg her to let him get out of this house. Odd, there was a time when this isolation would have delighted him. He was, indeed, a changed man thanks to her.

The following day, with the manuscript copy secured under his mattress, Eric called Greg. "Hello, Greg, this is

Eric. I was sorry to hear things didn't go well between you and Amy."

"What do you mean? We're engaged to be married next June. I didn't want to wait that long, but you know how women are with that June bride stuff."

"You're kidding? Why did you take Deedee out on New Years than?"

"What's going on over there, Eric? It's not as if you weren't invited."

"Oh?"

"Yeah. I was sorry to hear that you weren't able to get around yet. I told Deedee the wheelchair wouldn't pose a problem."

"I see. Well, maybe I'll be able to make it next time. Did Amy have a good time?"

"Hell, yes. She danced my legs off. Between her and Deedee, anyway."

"Well, don't be strangers. I wouldn't mind a little company once in a while. And, Greg, thanks."

"Thanks?"

"For showing Deedee a good time."

"Ah Ha!" Eric shouted aloud after he had hung up the phone. So, he wasn't the only one who could be deceitful. Maybe there was a chance for him after all. Maybe it was a new ball game, and he was up to bat.

CHAPTER SIXTEEN

Did Eric have any idea what he was doing to her? When she handed him his tray, he would touch her hand and send shivers vibrating through her. Deedee didn't know if this was some kind of new game he was playing, or if the touches were accidental. Perhaps, once again, she was simply a limp dishrag when she was near him.

The days were passing one by one like molasses. She didn't know if she could endure much more, but she had committed herself to this lunatic arrangement and really had no choice.

To make things worse, the weather had turned and the dogs were in more than they were out. That posed no problem with Cisco, but Samson was an enormous puppy who was methodically turning her house into a ramshackle mess. Once, when she was gone for groceries, he tore the leather cushions from her couch and proceeded to eat them. She came home to find stuffing carpeting her living room. Thank God, she had managed to rearrange the cushions to where the damage didn't show, but there would be no more rotating to avoid wear. The wear had already occurred.

After that happened, she had to make sure the puppy was locked in Eric's bedroom when she left the house. Usually, Samson was happy to lay by Eric's wheelchair while he drew his plans. Deedee had had to take over the taping and racking of his ears. Sometimes, she felt she was nursing the puppy more than she was Eric. She was certainly lavishing more love on the gangly beast. Because Eric could handle his own personal needs, all she really did was feed him, change his sheets, and wash his clothes.

There was one advantage to Eric's condition. Because of his lower profile in the wheelchair, she didn't have to look into his eyes. That made things much easier. Deedee could perform her tasks without thinking about the QUESTION, or the LOVEMAKING, or the HERMIT'S DEVIL EYES.

Time passed, breaking Deedee's heart a little with each ticking minute. On February seventh, the wheelchair rolled down the wooden ramp across the porch steps for only the second time. Eric had a doctor's appointment, and Deedee dutifully labored to shove the folded chair into the back seat of her tiny car. It was a miracle, but she finally rolled him into the waiting room.

A uniformed nurse took over from there and wheeled him into a cubicle to await the doctor. Deedee wanted to go there with him. No. That was something his fiancé, should do…or his wife. She picked up a thick magazine and tried uselessly to find something that would capture her attention.

An hour later, Eric came down the hall, towering to his full height with a crutch secured under each armpit. The cast for his broken ankle was gone, and a walking heel had been added to the leg cast. Deedee felt the crack of doom as the realization hit her. This would change her life dramatically. He no longer needed her. But, they had said it would take three months.

It wasn't that she needed the money. She never had. Had she? "Eric, you can walk!"

"Yeah. Isn't it great?"

"Well, of course," she lied.

"The ankle's still a little tender, but I can bear it."

"Are you going to leave the chair? Don't you think you'll still need it for awhile?"

"No. Don't worry, Deedee. I can make it to the car. It might be slow going, but I'll get used to it."

"I don't want you to fall again."

"I won't. I promise."

It WOULD be his right leg that was healed. He could easily drive now, drive away and leave her. Why should she care? If she wanted him, surely she would have said yes when he asked to marry her. Was her subconscious trying to tell her something? Was it better to keep her independence, and let Eric go? Wouldn't that solve all of her problems?

They didn't talk on the way home; each holding their own conversation in their minds. Eric made his way up the steps and into the house without her help. Hearing him mumbling through his closed door, Deedee wondered who he was calling. She had never heard him use the phone before. He usually used his fax instead.

She went to the kitchen to get out meat to thaw for dinner. Before she reentered the living room, the doorbell rang. "Amy, Greg, what are you doing here?"

Amy spoke out. "Is that any way to greet your friends? God, Deedee, Eric's turned you into more of a hermit than he is. Or have you always been?"

Typical that Amy would get under her skin so quickly. "You didn't answer my question."

Greg took the ball before Amy put it out of the ball park. "Eric called. He wants us to help him move back home."

Deedee was infuriated. "I moved him over here. I can certainly move him back."

Hearing the thunk of crutches to the hardwood floor, Deedee turned to see Eric enter the living room.

"Hi, guys. Thanks for coming," he said morbidly.

The doorbell rang again. Two men entered when Deedee opened it. "We're here to pick up a hospital bed."

Eric answered them. "It's in here," he said, pointing to the room behind him.

Deedee stomped off to the kitchen and clattered pots and pans. She threw the meat back into the freezer; it was far too much for one person. Still hearing activity in the other room, she put on a sweater that was hanging on a peg near the back door and went outside. Shivering, she sat on the back stoop and brooded while her life came apart.

After what seemed an eternity, the door at her back came open and Deedee turned. She looked up through the screen to see Eric standing there.

"Deedee, I wanted to thank you for all that you've done for me. I don't know how I could have managed without you."

Did she see his black eyes turn to sheets of silver through the fogging screen, or was that a trick of the light?

"Good-by, Deedee…and take care."

Then he was gone.

She waited a few minutes and went back into the house. Her computer was no longer in the dining room. Going into Eric's room, she found it in it's original position, girdled by files and shelves. The bed was gone. Eric's drawing table was gone, as was his fax and phone. The room was very empty, though it was filled with her things. Deedee didn't know if she would ever be able to write in there again. Too many memories lingered in every corner. A deep-timbre voice would echo to traumatize her.

She hadn't even said good-by to him. She had stared up at him as if he were some mysterious stranger spouting absurd nonsense. Going into her own bedroom, Deedee fell on the bed and cried for many hours. She cried to an empty house and an empty heart and felt the void within her that Eric had vacated—a void that no one else ever could fill.

The next day, a moving van arrived at the house next door. The Great Dane puppy disappeared from the back yard; the puppy she had grown to love. He had been named by her, from a very large dog in her novel about a very large man.

She watched from her window as Eric's jeep pulled out onto his driveway. He looked her way. Samson sat high in the passenger seat beside him. Eric looked extremely handsome in his cowboy hat which tipped in her direction.

Eric saw her standing behind the glass storm door.

Again, she saw him mouth the words as he had before. "I love you." Yes, she knew that now, without any doubt. And, she loved him, too, but it was the kind of love that you're afraid of—that consumes you in its fire and leaves nothing but a pile of ashes.

She felt like ashes, with no substance except the flaky residue of her miserable life. Eric was leaving. If it hadn't been for his injuries, he would have left long ago. He had been unable to tolerate her world any longer than she had tolerated his.

Her world—this frigid, rigid room—this was Daniel's world. She had just lived here with him—a tag along on his journey to fame and riches. How many times had she glanced around this room and hated it because of its lack of warmth? Poor Eric must have hated staying here after his snug cabin. SHE hated living here after HER snug cabin.

She walked out onto her front porch after the van trundled down the street. Watching it until it could no longer be seen, she turned to go back into her emptiness. She saw her casserole dish beside the door resting atop her novel "Tall Timbre". Lifting them both, she wondered why he had left the book.

When she held it loosely in her hands, it naturally fell open to the dedication. It was so easy to find a well-read passage. Each book revealed the will of its reader.

A note was scribbled under the dedication.

—To Eric and Big Dog, masters of the wild heart,
Love, Deedee—
—Deedee, you ARE the wild heart!
Love Forever, Eric—

She moved to sit on the couch and laid the book open on the coffee table. The weight of the book snapped it closed. Reopening it, she placed the heavy, crystal coaster on the spine.

Staring at his words for many hours, Deedee perused her heart. What did she want from life if not this man and his mountain? She had never been able to erase him from her mind. Her insides quivered and ached every waking moment without him. Yes, she had lost control of her "self" and independence when she was with him. Unresisting, he could mold her into any form he wanted. It had frightened her to know that someone—the hermit—could turn her into his love slave.

But Deedee was a slave to his love. It had happened. She couldn't undo the deed. Had it been so awful? Everything she had ever written had become reality in one rapturous explosion on his bed. He was a stick of dynamite, and she had lit his fuse. Should she abandon him, again, to let the tumbling boulders bury him on his mountain?

"I love you, Eric. God, I've been so self-centered and stupid. No one has ever put me on a pedestal. I was afraid I would fall and no one would be there to catch me."

Was it too late? Had she destroyed all of the happiness they had shared. No one could ever fill this empty place in her heart except him. Without him, it would eat away at her like a cancer. She had to try. She had to tell him. Her love for him was bigger than the mountain, bigger than Big Dog, and bigger than her silly illusions of independence.

What was independence, anyway, except a fancy word for loneliness. Dependence meant you needed someone to make your life complete, and she needed Eric. Spoiled by his sharing of her home, she had thought that things would go on perpetually without making waves in her life. But he was gone. It had taken his absence to bring the truth crashing down on Deedee. She couldn't live without this man and didn't really even want to.

"God, don't let it be too late."

There was so much to do. Her house would have to be put up for sale. All of her assets would have to be transferred to Jones and Breyer Associates, Colorado Springs, Colorado. She had to go shopping. Yes. That would be perfect.

* * * * * * *

The little car wouldn't pull the trailer up the last hill. It turned the snow to glass as the smoking tire tried to bite. Deedee humphed and got out of the car. She let Cisco run ahead of her and carried Poncho snuggled against her side. Her train got caught on a snaggy, winter weed, and she yanked it to dislodge it, ripping the fine net.

Samson ran up to her. His unbound ears were standing to perfection. He pounced on her, and his muddy-snowy paws left trails down her white satin skirt. She saw the cabin and started screaming his name.

Eric started up from the screams of a Banshee. He had been working, and his table went flying from his excited exit. He ran through the house, as fast as he could go with the cumbersome crutches, and threw open the front door.

A snow-white woman was trudging across the snow-white ground. Samson and Cisco circled her, barking in bounding joy. A wedding veil sat cockeyed on her fiery hair, and her satin train dragged an angel trail through the fresh snow. Two muddy paw marks testified that Samson had claimed her for his own.

"Oh, no you don't, Dog." Eric gimped from the shelter of the porch and tore up the ground to reach her. He heard her scream of delight mixed with concern when he tripped and sprawled on the cold ground.

As Eric looked up into sparkling blue eyes, he heard the illusion speak. "I AM the wild heart, and YOU are my master. I love you, Eric. Why haven't I ever told you so?"

Deedee fell to her knees before him, dragging his crutches from the deep snow. He captured her, and Poncho squirmed between them. They rolled in the snow, kissing, staring deeply into eyes they thought they would never see again, screaming their joy to the top of their mountain.

Eric pinned her down. "God, Deedee, I never want to tame that wild heart of yours. Love is our master."

THE END

ABOUT THE AUTHOR

Tish Hand works as a graphic designer at a t-shirt shop called Tee's Etc. in Enid, Oklahoma. She is an award-winning artist and has portraits worldwide. She tries her skill at everything and has accomplished classical guitar, carpentry, plumbing, electrical, mechanics, computer technology, monogramming, and creating pageant dresses for her granddaughter. Her hobbies include singing karaoke, playing Tomb Raider, and boating with her fiancé, Larry Humphrey. The boys usually come with them. They are Chewy, a Lhaso Apso, who is the boss, and his bigger, younger, but not wiser companion, Mojo, who was saved from being road kill by Larry while going down a local highway.

Widowed after thirty-two years of married life, she has three grown children, and four grandchildren, all of whom she is very proud.